The Pirouette Predator

by

Jade Lee Wright

Dedication

I dedicate this book to wine, salt & vinegar crisps, true crime podcasts and trashy reality television – all of which kept me sane in between writing this.

This book is also dedicated to Corona Virus / Covid-19... because without a world pandemic giving me no more excuses to procrastinate against writing, I finally finished this novel! My heart goes out to everyone affected by this virus.

I'd also like to personally thank the My Favorite Murder Facebook group, Drinkerino's. All of your love and support completely overwhelmed me. You are family.
Thank you to Jocelyn Blouin, my coffee addict friend who has always believed in my writing and supported me in every step I take.

Time heals all wounds, they say.
I say they just have to fester a little bit first; and fester, they did.

CHAPTER 1

Dread twists my stomach into knots as my car winds its way down the familiar mountain pass. Years have passed since I've returned home, yet absolutely nothing has changed. That's the thing about small towns, I guess.

The same rusty signs covered in bullet holes and graffiti stand askew, welcoming me back.

The same broken fencing along the side of the potholed road still hasn't been fixed.

Sluggishly, my car pulls to a stop in front of the only traffic light in town. I breathe in deeply, my eyes focusing on the arum lilies that litter the overgrown fields.

I don't want to be here.

I already miss the city. The hustle and bustle. The smog. The old Gothic buildings guarded by gargoyles and the sound of the traffic.

When the light flicks to green my engine sputters to life, struggling in the icy winter morning.

My fingers grip the steering wheel tighter.

The Honda emblem shines into my eyes as I turn the corner onto Hazel Street.

Everything I own in life is crammed into the cardboard boxes piled up on the back seat.

Clothes and books mainly. An impressive collection of coffee mugs.

I've never had much. Never needed much.

Michael and I had bought everything together. The bed, the coffee table, my timber writing desk. Bookshelves, wine racks, rugs. Even coat-hangers. The three-seater sofa he positioned in front of the wide screen television so he could watch sport and play X-box.

Everything was *ours*.

There was never a question about what belonged to whom.

He doesn't realise that he's taken everything. Left me with nothing.

He's probably curled up on that sofa we both paid for, right now, with *her*.

Memories I try to avoid lurch into my head.

My heart hammers as I pull into my sisters driveway. The keys are cold and heavy in my hands as I trudge up to the front door. There's a build up of mail that I gather up and drop on the console table once I'm inside. Dust greets me, nothing more.

There's a dank smell, like no one's been here for a while. No windows are open to let the fresh air in.

I kick a rock in front of the door and start lugging my boxes inside one by one. I can't quite bear to unpack them yet. It's too hard.

Instead, I wander through the hallway, staring at the framed photographs that travel along the wall. It's a strange feeling looking at a photo of you and your sister and not being able to tell the difference. We are completely identical and yet nothing alike. It should be easier to tell us apart.

Robyn does ballet and while I'm just as dainty as her, I've never been able to dance.

I take a black and white photograph of her in a leotard, her willowy body stretched across the stage. She looks weightless. The girl in the picture looks just like me, yet couldn't possibly be. I sigh and return the frame to its hook. I touch the glass and whisper, '*where are you?*'

It's the first time I've spoken in days and my voice shocks me. It breaks an unsettling silence, sending shivers down my spine.

I'd sent Robyn a message days ago letting her know that I was coming to visit. I didn't think it necessary to go into the gritty details of my breakup. That could be done over a bottle of Riesling on her porch.

She'd never responded to my message which wasn't like her but I had no where else to go so I'd packed up my life and left my ex fiancé's house for good.

Every time I think about it, it guts me. I've been trying so hard to push my feelings aside. Ignore them. That's my coping mechanism, never dealing with the situation head on.

Eventually the pain will fade if I pretend it isn't there for long enough, right?

I look through the rest of Robyn's cottage for some kind of sign of her.

An old ballet barre she's using as decoration is coated in dust. There's an entire wall where her old, worn in pointe shoes are dangling, some speckled with blood, showing her years of hard work in the dance industry. She used to go through a couple of pairs of those shoes a week.

She's always had a thing for plants. The sunflower sitting on her kitchen windowsill has perished. The leaves from her bonsai have withered and fallen off. A creeper plant trailing down her bookshelf is the only thing still alive but the soil in the pot is bone dry.

There's an old copy of Anna Karenina on her night-stand. The spine is cracked and one of the pages is dog-eared.

My sisters nose used to always be buried in a book if she wasn't dancing.

I flick through the book until I find something highlighted.

It says, '*Love. The reason I dislike that word is that it means too much for me, far more than you can understand*.'

My eyebrows furrow as I place the book back down.

I sit on her bed. The sheets have a subtle lingering smell of her perfume. I breathe her in, hold my breath.

I haven't been here for a while but it doesn't seem like anything is missing. There isn't a gap in her wardrobe where clothes should be. Her Burberry travel bag is stuffed away on the top shelf.

In the bathroom, all of her toiletries are there. Full bottles of TRESemmé shampoo and conditioner stand in her shower.

I wander back out into the lounge area and pluck at the strings of her ukelele, abandoned to one side of her sofa. It's horrifically out of tune. She used to post so many video clips onto her Instagram account, playing it. I pull up her page now, just to check. She hasn't been active for a while.

River barks at something outside, her shaggy tail wagging nervously in this strange, new environment.

I trip on a crack in the tiles on my way to the window. This place needs a lot of work. Tree roots have lifted the flooring, mould has spread over the walls and cobwebs dangle from every corner.

Outside, someone's got their hands on my rusted car door, peering into the window. My skin prickles.

Grabbing River's leash, I attach it to her collar and march outside. The man by my car instantly straightens up, his eyes darting from me to my dog.

"Robyn! You're back. Where the hell have you been?" he booms in an overly friendly voice.

River snarls as he strides towards me. The hair on her back stands on end. His grin is too wide, showing a full set of veneers.

He's on the larger side, pale blue jeans straining around his waist and a collared shirt missing a number of buttons. The teeth don't suit the rest of his appearance.

"Who's this then?" the man asks, smiling down at my dog.

"River."

"Robyn and River, love it!"

"I'm not-" I start, but he's already bending down, offering a hand out for River to sniff. She does so cautiously but doesn't seem to warm to him like she usually does with new people.

When he stands back up he tries to pull me into a hug.

"I'm not Robyn," I say, taking a step back.

He laughs at this.

"Very funny. You've had everyone worried sick," he says loftily.

"I'm *not* Robyn," I repeat, this time more firmly.

He squints in the sunlight as he looks me over. It takes a few seconds for the realisation to sink in.

"Jesus... Piper?"

I nod slowly.

"Piper Brady... never thought you'd be back in this hell hole of a town again!" he chuckles.

"I'm sorry, who are you?"

"Cody. We were in pre-school together way back when!"

I can't place his features but nod again.

"You probably hear this all the time, but it's insane how much you look like Rob!" his eyes are looking me over with fascination.

You get used to that when you're a twin.

"Still here then?" I ask, not meaning for it to come out the way that it does.

A lot of people who grow up here never leave. I was one of the lucky ones, I suppose.

Even though I can see him trying to hide it, I can tell my comment has offended him.

"Robyn and I work together at the high school. She hasn't shown up for a while so I thought I'd swing by to see if she's OK?" he peers over my shoulder to the cottage as if trying to catch a glimpse of her.

"How long has she been missing?" I ask. I don't know why I choose the word '*missing*.'

It sounds alien and unnecessary on my tongue.

Why hadn't I used the word, '*gone*?'

She can't be missing... she's just wandered off again.

"Well, she's buggered off for a few days before here and there but she always prances back in like nothing ever happened. This time it's been weeks. I've been here a few times to check in but this is the first time I saw someone parked outside. There's been absolutely no word from her and I'm sorry to say it, the school needs to start looking for a new teacher now. She's chanced her luck enough, you know? When she does come back, she's getting immediately dismissed," he hands me an envelope addressed to her.

I let his words sink in, calcify.

Weeks.

It has been weeks since anyone last saw my sister... and no one told me.

*

Coffee burns my throat as I take my tablets the next morning. I long since stopped punching the pills out of the blister pack one by one. Now I toss a palm full of medication into my mouth all at once.

I grimace as I swallow, wondering to myself why the hell I still bother taking birth control on top of everything else. I'm at that stage in a breakup where if I never have sex again, I think I'd be OK with it. I can't imagine being with anyone else, starting anew. Learning someone and letting someone learn me from scratch. Telling the same awful stories from my life I'd shared with Michael. A repeat, just with fresh ears. What's the point?

All these drugs, yet nothing works quite as well as nicotine.

I bring the cigarette to my lips and let the menthol fill my lungs. Everything about the way Robyn's cottage has been left makes it look like she'd just popped out for a walk or something. While I was scratching around earlier, I discovered her handbag. It had everything in it she'd need if she was going away. Her drivers license, bank card, passport – but what really shook me was the packet of pills.

We're on the same medication. Without it, things can spiral out of control very quickly.

It's when I saw the pills that things cemented in place for me. Something is really wrong.

She's been missing for forty-nine days and counting. Holding the poster with her face emblazoned on it above the bold MISSING text is surreal.

I'm so confused.

We always had that odd twin connection. We could be oceans apart but if she was down, or vice versa, we'd feel it. No matter where we were in the world, if she was craving pizza then so was I. Some call it telepathy.

Now, I feel nothing. There's just this numbing, empty space where my sister once was.

Navigating my way through life without feeling her running through my veins is the strangest sensation in the world.

I really don't want to think of her as dead but her sudden disappearance both physically and mentally has me suspecting the worst.

If something has happened to her – rape, abduction or God forbid, murder, I'd like to think I'd sense that.

Instead, it's like she was never there at all. Very much like Michael. My best friend, my lover. It's like he died but worse, because he didn't. He chose to leave me.

The loss of both my sister and Michael is too much for me to comprehend.

I'm not holding it together. It's too much all at once. Not my sister. Not the man I was certain I was going to spend the rest of my life with.

Please, no.

A tear rolls down my cheek.

I sit on the stool while I wait for my meds to kick in, pulling hard on my cigarette. I knock back the rest of my coffee.

After putting up posters on a dozen lampposts I stop at the high school. Cody wants me to chat to the headmaster about helping out while Robyn's '*away*.'

Her energy here is overwhelming. Flowers and cards decorate her classroom. Gifts are stacked up on her desk and messages from the students are scrawled across her chalkboard.

I read them all, holding yellow chalk between my fingers, trying to think of what to write. I feel like I should leave something there but there are no words. I'm so deep in thought that I don't even notice when I snap the chalk in two.

I spin the globe that sits atop her desk. As the countries and oceans blur together the door behind me opens.

"You made it," Cody smiles meekly as he too takes in the room.
"I really don't think I'm what the students want..." I try, pointing
out that people will probably get spooked out seeing their missing
teachers identical twin sister. Plus, I can't teach dance! It's
laughable. I could teach them art or acting and theory but not how
to prance around in revealing pink lycra.
"Nonsense. Come on, interview time," he winks.

*

The interview went well, considering. Robyn and I both studied
teaching and with the school in dire need of a new drama teacher
I was their first port of call. I agreed to be a substitute until my
sister comes home.
Both Cody and the headmaster looked at me with sympathy when
I said that. It made me feel stupid. Naive.

I wake at around 2am again. I don't even need to check my watch
anymore.
Robyn's spare room is suffocating, soulless.
I pad into the living room and stir River who, enviously, was
sleeping peacefully. She follows closely at my heels as we walk
through the garden in the dark. It's so cold that there's frost on the
grass. My sweatpants get sopping wet as I circle a tree,
contemplating the day ahead. It's my first day teaching Robyn's
kids.
I've had my teaching qualification for years but I've never used it.
The only reason I studied was because Robyn hadn't wanted to
study alone. As free-spirited as she is, it always amazed me how
much she thought she couldn't do without me by her side.
I always knew I'd head off and work overseas – earn the big
bucks. The day I'd left we'd both cried but I knew her separation
anxiety was so much worse than mine.
I watch my breath drift off in the darkness, bundling myself up in
my plum coloured throw-over.
Once River's back indoors I lock up, boil the kettle and switch the

lights on in the bedroom.

I choose an outfit, a simple pencil skirt, a collared shirt and a pair of black leather pumps. I have to laugh at how professional I look when I glance in the mirror.

She was halfway through creating a ballet show when she disappeared.

To be honest I'd rather be spending my time turning over every stone to find her than teaching a bunch of hormonal teenagers.

Sadly though, Michael took every penny I ever had when he left me so I need this job, badly.

From the moment I enter the classroom I know this isn't going to be easy.

Over twenty pairs of eyes ogle at me as I make my way to the desk.

They've been warned that I'm their teachers identical twin sister but nothing can quite prepare you for seeing a ghost.

I try to get on with the class, get to know the students and their roles in their current production but they all seem more fascinated by me.

All they can see is my sister when they look at me. I can't blame them for being shaken up.

I ask them if I can watch what they've been working on with Robyn and we all head to the hall.

Everything changes when they get onto stage. I see a beautiful side to each and every one of them, their passion and talent.

There's two girls and one guy that really stand out to me. They are absolute naturals. Fluid, authentic and excellent.

Chloe, Bibiana and Luke.

I make a mental note to keep my eye on all three of them.

It's Luke that surprises me the most. He's a virtuoso in dance.

He carries the entire class and gives more guidance than even I do. I feel quite inadequate in comparison.

I wonder what Robyn thought *(thinks)* of him.

I hate that I'm starting to use the past tense when I talk about her.

There's been absolutely no progress with Robyn's case. It's like she's just vanished off of the face of the earth. My connection with her has been severed.

CHAPTER 2

I immerse myself into teaching. Into watching Luke plié around me in his canvas slippers.

It would help if he wasn't so attractive. It would also help if certain appendages were more covered up but his ballet tights hug his thighs and leave nothing up to the imagination. I can make out every single muscle in his body.

Those baby blue eyes and five o'clock shadow along his jawline makes me weak.

His height, his chiselled body, athletic but thin. His perfect posture.

Cody's noticed the way I cross my legs a little too tightly when Luke comes onto the stage; but I couldn't care less about what Cody thinks. He's always lurking around, trying to engage in conversation with me.

I catch him staring sometimes, looking at me during lunch or in meetings but especially when Luke is around us. It's ridiculous, Luke is over a decade younger than me.

A girl can dream though...

I've noticed myself putting more effort into my appearance, dabbing extra concealer under my eyes and blush across my cheekbones.

I'm trying to make myself believe it isn't all for Luke but if I'm honest, I am trying to hide my new found wrinkles more than I usually would. He's the kind of guy you can't help but want to impress. When he smiles at me or looks at me from under those long eyelashes, I feel special.

He's told me I look nice a few times in the morning before dancing. Before all of the other students arrive.

The first time he'd said it, it was so casual while he was dusting a box filled with pointe shoes with rosin.

I'm embarrassed to admit how much I like it when he says things like that. It makes me feel young again. Alive.

On the other hand, it makes me feel so deflated when he *doesn't* notice.

I run to the bathroom and inspect my face in the mirror, smeared with other girls lipstick kisses.

I've become so judgemental about myself and my age – but at the same time it's given me something new to focus on instead of Robyn and Michael. Where she is. What he did.

I have this determination to be beautiful again instead of not caring like the last few months.

It's given me a drive to try harder. A new lease on life, as they say. I wish Robyn were here. I do think of her daily.

I'm worried sick to my stomach and feeling useless because there's literally nothing I can do right now to help her.

If she were here we could compare our ageing. Where she has a freckle, I have a freckle. We're not mirror image twins. We are completely identical. It's a wonder our fingerprints aren't a perfect match. I miss her so much.

The bell rings, allowing the students to drop whatever it is they're doing and head off to their next lesson.

I head over to the costume room and start to spray freshener on the clothing dangling from the racks. It's nice to be able to turn the blaring classical music off and enjoy silence for a while.

I'm unfastening my bun when Luke flops down in a chair beside me.

"Did you see what I did in Act Two? I really think that should be incorporated into the show," he says, draping a long arm over my shoulder.

His skin is soft and fervent against my own. The feeling is electrifying.

I haven't been touched since the day I crawled, snivelling into Michael's arms when we were saying our final goodbyes.

Luke is unfamiliar, exciting.

It makes me emotional, remembering the visceral fear I had the day Michael told me there was nothing I could do to fix us.

I blink back the tears and lean into Luke, eager to smell his cologne. I don't want him to see me cry.

I know it's wrong but I can't stop myself.

Before I know it, his fingers skim over my shoulders. I'm instantly aroused.

I don't know where this has come from but I'm amazed that he wants *me*.

He could have whoever he wants and right now, that's me.

Grateful that the last student closed the door behind her I allow him to lift me off of my feet.

It's effortless and I can feel his biceps bulging beneath my hands.

My chest rises and falls quickly, his hands cup my chin. He brings my lips to his, a hint of guava on his breath.

It doesn't take long for my clothes to fall to the ground.

I don't care if we get caught, in this moment nothing else matters.

This is bad. It's wrong. It's completely dizzying.

He puts me into positions I never thought possible but the moment is ephemeral, over too soon.

Thank God for those birth control tablets after all.

*

Robyn doesn't stay as front page news for long.

Today there's a photograph of another girl, a student.

The word MISSING dominates the page followed by what she was last seen wearing.

She has a scar across her collarbone from an old surgery, a beauty spot at the corner of her left eye.

I fold the newspaper back up and thrum my fingers on the hardwood table.

This is the fifth disappearance in the span of three months.

For a town as small as ours, this is terrifying. How are all of these girls just vanishing?

Parents of the missing girls have all given statements assuring people that their daughters would never run off and make them worry like this.

At first there wasn't much concern for Robyn. People have always known her to be a free-spirit, someone who could never live by the book.

It was only when others started getting poached that she became a potential victim too.

After all, they all had certain similarities. They all danced.

There were no striking resemblances in their appearances like brunette hair parted down the middle the way Ted Bundy liked – it was their incredible talent for dancing that connected the dots.

Some articles compared whoever has been taking these girls to Rodney Alcala, who used to pretend to be a professional photographer and target women who would model for him.

That was one theory, anyway.

Another comparison that made headlines was The Beauty Queen Killer, Christopher Wilder.

People's imaginations were running wild.

I scratch around in my purse, finding just enough coins to pay for my peanut-butter smoothie.

River bolts up beside me at the sound of her leash being picked up.

We wander aimlessly down the street, bustling with weekend traffic. I still get mistaken for Robyn sometimes.

People wave through their car windows at me or stop me in my tracks.

It's incredible how many people have forgotten that she has a twin sister. There's an awkward pause when they realise who I am – or rather, who I'm not.

They try to ask me about the progress in my sisters case but they soon find their excuses to wrap the conversation up.

River tugs me along the pavement, sniffing around in every direction.

It's a freezing day. The mountains in the distance have snowcapped peaks that I'm sure the students are all going to see this weekend.

We bump into Cody further up the road.

You can't go anywhere in a small town without seeing someone you know.

He looks different out of his work attire. More relaxed.

He's wearing a woollen cardigan over a dark blue shirt and corduroy pants.

He tries his luck winning River over by crouching down to her level.

In his hand there's a bottle of Merlot. The liquid sloshes around as he asks me what my plans are for the weekend.

"Not much at all," I say, vaguely.

"Well, I'm not going to drink this all myself," he waves the bottle at me, smiling glibly.

I on the other hand, could easily drink a bottle of wine to myself.

"Fancy popping over later for a winter warmer?"

This is possibly his seventh attempt at trying to get me over to his place. I've lost count.

I'm starting to wonder if he used to have a thing for my sister.

The way he looks at me gives me the creeps.

I'm running out of excuses to turn him down, so instead I sigh.

"Why not."

I'd prefer to have my legs wrapped around Luke's head but I think Cody's cottoning on to my inappropriate relationship with him.

He seems genuinely thrilled that I've finally accepted his offer.

He strolls through the graveyard with us on the way up to his place.

The town is built around one the largest graveyards I've ever seen.

There's a bigger population of the dead here than the living.

He pours a generous amount of wine which he brings out onto the balcony and sits down beside me. I sip the merlot gratefully as he passes me a blanket to wrap around myself.

We sit in an awkward silence for a moment as I take in the view of crumbling tombstones and open graves waiting to be filled.

I can't help but wonder if one of them will one day be for my sister.

*

"Can I ask you something?" I say once I've had two glasses of wine. I can feel myself easing up, relaxing.

"Shoot."

"Why haven't you ever left?"

He pours me another glass of wine, frowning at my question.

He brings his glass up to his lips but doesn't take a sip. I notice his ring finger.

The skin is lighter around it.

I feel like I'm prying.

"Why have I never left? Honestly? Let myself go a bit," he pats his belly. I scoff at this.

"But also, even after my wife left me... this is a big reason," he points at the bottle of wine he'd bought earlier. I cock my head to one side in question.

"We're in one of the best wine regions in the world!" his eyes light up as he picks up the bottle. It's only then I realise the date on the label. 1989.

I don't think I've ever seen a date on a wine bottle go that far back.

"I know absolutely nothing about wine, really," I laugh, peering down at the garnet coloured liquid in my glass.

"What is this, for example?" I point down to the last bit of wine. It looks like there's sand in the glass. I've seen it before but I've always ignored it.

"That's sediment or, as some people call it, wine dregs or crystals. A lot of people think it's bad but it's the complete opposite. It's a sign that the wine is really high quality," he swirls the last few drops around in the glass.

"So it's harmless?" I feel clueless.

"Yes," he chuckles.

"Why did you choose this bottle specifically?"

He picks the bottle up.

"This is a 1989 Meerlust Merlot," he says, twisting the bottle this way and that.

"It's one of my favourite vintage wines. Do you like it?" he asks shyly.

"I do," I nod, taking a sip. It feels velvety on my tongue.

I still don't quite taste a huge difference between this one and the usual glass of wine I order in a pub with dinner but I don't tell him that.

"Probably cost a lot with a date like that?"

"Just over a thousand..."

I choke, looking up at him in disbelief.

"A thousand!? You're not serious?"

We're sitting around an old oak wine barrel watching the sun go down. Sunsets are always best in winter here.

He clears his throat, a slight smile playing on his lips. I'd never noticed how plump they are before.

"How do you afford that?" I ask, acutely aware of our teachers salaries.

"Some people budget for a fancy car they can show off or save up to have a nice holiday. I budget for good wine."

I sigh, wanting to get off of the topic of money.

He must pick up my unease as he switches back to talking about the sediment in our glasses.

"You get two types of sediment. This one is called colloids. You can tell because it's quite fine. It has a grainier texture, you see?" he brings the glass up close so I can take a good look.

I can see the teacher in him as he talks.

He's patient and softly spoken, easy to listen to.

"The easiest way to explain it is to say it's a protein. It's leftover remnants of the grapes skin and seeds. When wine gets filtered it takes the sediment out and basically robs the wine of a lot of its flavour and mouth-feel."

"So you never just go to the shops and pick a cheap bottle off the shelf then?"

"Only to cook with," he grins.

I think of the bottles on my wine rack back at the cottage. They're all cheap and cheerful.

I've never even considered buying a bottle that costs more than filling my car up with a tank of petrol! I never really saw the point of it. Expensive wine has always been wasted on someone like me.

I take another sip with a new found sense of appreciation.

"You said there's two types of sediment?" I ask, genuinely wanting to learn more.

It feels nice to take my mind off of everything for an hour or two.

"Yeah. So the other one is called tartrate. Sounds like I'm giving you a science lesson or something," he laughs.

I smile back at him, listening to the sound of the crickets all around us.

"Tartrates are bigger than colloids. Remember these are colloids because they're sand-like. Tartrates are more like diamonds, if you will. They get formed when tartaric acid connects with potassium in cold weather conditions. It makes a crystalline salt formation and has a tendency to stick to the cork or sides of the bottle so when you pour it into a glass it can cling onto the sides of the glass, too."

"You lost me at potassium! How do you know all this stuff?" I ask, bemused.

"I like wine."

"Impressive!"

"If I wasn't a teacher I'd definitely become a winemaker. Maybe one day," he says whimsically.

A salty breeze from the lagoon drifts by and I catch a waft of his aftershave. I quite like it.

"You know, this town, as boring as you might think it is, is home."

I never understood people who have no desire to leave.

I have no right to feel sorry for him if he's truly happy here, but I do.

Just like Robyn. I always wanted her to get out. Do something with her life. Make something of herself... but she was always so content with staying somewhere familiar and teaching.

Maybe her and Cody are more alike than I originally realised.

"I'm sorry – I don't know why I asked you that," I say, feeling bad.

"Don't be. I get it. Once you've had a taste of the world you don't want to be in a place like this."

He's right. While it feels like I've been to more countries than I can count, neither him or my sister have ever left South Africa. A part of me is using Cody to understand my sisters way of life.

"Were you close with her?" I ask him.

"Robyn? No!" he laughs.

"She was never interested in me, why would she be?" He gestures to himself. My heart breaks for him.

I flounder for something to say in return.

I find myself actually warming to Cody throughout the night. I may not be the best judge of character but he seems harmless.

On my way to the bathroom I stumble upon framed photographs from his wedding day. I'm stunned that they're all still up on the wall.

He looks... different. Almost handsome.

I look at his ex wife, studying her face. She's beautiful. I wonder where she is now.

We have another glass of wine each, snacking on olives and a selection of cheese he's brought out for us on a wooden chopping board.

He tells me how good of a teacher Robyn was to the kids. He talks about how passionate he could tell she was about dance.

"I'd often come to the hall and watch the show coming together. She really was very talented," he smiles.

Was.

I can picture him sitting in the back of the hall in the dark, watching my sister.
I wonder if she ever noticed. I wonder if it made her uncomfortable at all.
"She still is talented," I bristle, feeling the mood of the evening darken.

The quickest way back to my sisters house is through the graveyard.
Cody tells me he thinks he should walk me home but I tell him I'll be fine with River.
I quickly gulp down the last of the wine so I can leave.
He's not happy about me walking alone and makes me put his number on speed dial.
I'm slightly tipsy after drinking on an empty stomach so the walk home is a bit hazy.
River pisses on someone's grave obliviously and I stumble on guiltily.
Crickets and frogs sing through the starless night. I can barely see my hand in front of me there's so much fog.
Robyn and I always used to come out here late at night to share a bottle of brandy. We would smuggle the alcohol out of our foster parents liquor cabinet and feel so rebellious.
I find the spot beneath our favourite tree and sit down on a log.
I still feel this unexplainable nothingness.
I was hoping that by coming here it would trigger something in me but it doesn't work.
I wonder if this is how the rest of the world feels. As a twin I've never felt 'alone' until now.
My sister and I were together from day one, sharing the same amniotic sac. Now there's nothing but a yawning chasm where she once was.
River pants by my side. I tickle behind her ears to calm her. She's on high alert.
The wine is dizzying me so I take a moment to lean back against the tree and close my eyes. I let the breeze wrap around me and

slowly, I drift away.

I wake with a start. I can hear footsteps close by, twigs snapping underfoot.
Dawn is just starting to break.
I keep dead still but River whines nervously next to me.
My eyes dart around but it's still too dark to see anything properly.
The footsteps grow closer, louder, faster. I hold my breath.
"What on earth are you doing out here?"
It's a voice I don't recognise.
I'm frozen with panic, unable to speak.
A man emerges from the darkness and stands over me.
"Christ alive, thought you were one of them girls who've been missing. Thought you were dead!" There's a rusted shovel in his hand which he sees me eyeing cautiously.
"You alright there?" His skin is leathery and his lips cracked.
He's trembling, sickly looking.
I nod and scramble to my feet.
"Dangerous for a pretty woman like you to be out here all alone," he stabs the shovel into the earth and leans on it languidly.
"I was just leaving," I croak, taking a few steps around him. River trots next to me.
My head is throbbing from the wine.
I blink back the black spots that blur my vision.
He's wearing dark blue overalls which makes me think he must be the grounds-keeper.
"Shouldn't be here alone," he mutters, shaking his head repeatedly.
I tell him I'm sorry, watching his tongue sliver over his scraggly moustache.
"Suffer little children who walk on my grave..." the man hisses after me. My skin crawls.
I hurry away, my head pounding.
Low hanging branches lacerate my arms as I fight my way to the gate leading out of the graveyard.

When I reach my sisters place I fall to my knees and sob. I cry for everything I've been holding in for weeks. I cry for my sister and for the other missing girls. I cry for Michael and for all of the hurt he has caused. I cry for my stack of unopened boxes filled with everything that reminds me of the life I used to have.

When I've finally pulled myself together I text Luke.
I just want to feel something. I crave the feeling of being desired. He sends me his address and tells me to come over. I knew he would.
His place is immaculate.
I'm impressed that someone his age has a place like this.
There's a lot of rustic wooden furniture, vintage leather seats and animal skin rugs. It's simple but classy.
There's a black and white portrait of Dame Ninette de Valois by his liquor cabinet. I'd recognise her anywhere.
She was the founder of Royal Ballet back in the thirties. I'm impressed he has something so special up on his wall. He really must have a deep-rooted passion for ballet.
I tease him about two bright floral pillows that he insists his mother bought him as a house-warming gift. They look atrociously out of place.
At first glance the place seems too good to be true but as I wander around I start noticing little things here and there. There's no hand-soap in the guest bathroom and most of the cupboards are bare.
I open his fridge and have to laugh. There's one unopened low-carb beer at the top and a plate with a huge half-eaten lamb knuckle on it.
There are a few bottles of different hot sauce and a small carton of almond milk that's out of date. I want to ask him where all his stuff is but he comes up behind me and starts planting kisses down my neck. I let him lead me to the bedroom.

I'm cupping his balls in my hand and listening to him groan into my hair.

It's still weird touching another man after years of being with Michael.

Luke's dick is smaller. Not bad, but definitely smaller.

It's an awful feeling to be disappointed in its size.

At least he knows how to use it.

I wonder when the memory of Michael's body will disintegrate. I wish it would hurry up.

Comparison is the thief of joy, as Theodore Roosevelt once said.

Having only been with one guy for so many years, it's hard for me not to compare.

Luke is nothing like Michael. He's barely got any hair on him.

I'd often run my fingers through Michael's hair while I lay on his chest, my head slowly moving up and down with his breathing.

Luke doesn't even have hair on his legs. He's chiselled and toned, he doesn't have the slight beer belly Michael was always complaining about.

It's a body so young and foreign to me. I don't actually know if I like it.

Luke nips at my neck, jolting me back into the present moment.

He runs his baby soft hands down my back, across my hips and lands his fingers right on my clit.

He starts to rub vigorously until I quake into him.

My orgasm is fierce, angry. So much pent up frustration releases from me in uncontrollable spasms.

I gasp, clawing at his sweaty back while he flips me onto my stomach and squirts all over my bare back.

I collapse onto my stomach over the damp sheets, stained with us.

It felt hurried, quick. Just what I needed.

He grabs his t-shirt and wipes his warm juices off of me.

He isn't a cuddler, which I'm strangely happy with. I'm not really ready to get affectionate with another guy in that way yet.

He can be incredibly affectionate before and during sex, but when it's over he jumps up and moves on to something else.

Now he heads into the shower. The steam leaks through the door, slowly filling his bedroom. It steams up his windows so I can't see outside.

I roll over, content in his bed, enjoying the smell of sex on my skin.

Like most of his house, his room is pristine despite the mangled bedsheets.

I'm so curious about him that I can't quite help myself when I peep into his bedside cabinet.

I recognise it immediately, the pink leather embossed with her initials.

R.I.B.

Robyn Isabella Brady.

I touch the gilded edges of my sisters journal. It was hidden beneath old receipts, ripped open condom wrappers and a packet of sleeping tablets.

I can hear Luke humming in the shower, scrubbing himself clean of me.

I take the book out and open it up.

There's a message written in the middle of the first page, a note from our last foster mother.

I have the same message in my own journal that looks exactly the same.

'Journalling is like whispering to one's self and listening at the same time,' - Mina Murray, Dracula.

Robyn wrote in her journal more than me. The pages are full of her swirly writing in black pen.

I fan the pages through to the last entry, dated just over four months ago.

I'm reading fast. The writing isn't as neat as it is on the previous pages.

I catch sight of Luke's name, of the words, '*I can't do this anymore.*'

The geyser jolts violently as Luke turns the shower off. I gasp, drop the book back and slam the drawer closed, my breath hitched.

I wrestle my way into my clothes which were strewn around the room.

I'm pulling on my boots when the bathroom door opens. He's stagnant in front of me, a towel hanging loosely on his bony hips. He leans over me, so closely I can see the iridescent colours in his eyes.

I want to scream, to demand an explanation.

What have you done to my sister?! But I am mute. Frozen.

His breath is hot against my skin.

His touch I found so debilitating just minutes ago now repulses me.

I'm shocked by the sting as his big open hand connects with my side.

He squeezes my love-handle, hard. His look is menacing, not flirtatious at all.

"You'd better get going," he says, freeing me.

I vault out of his house as fast as my shaking legs will allow.

*

River pants anxiously, nestled between my legs as I stare out of the window.

I haven't left the sofa for hours.

I should go to the police, get a search warrant. Find my sister.

The thing is, I *know* the police here. They'll seize her journal as evidence and forget about it.

They'll probably end up losing it.

It will disappear just like she did.

They'll question him, he'll lie. They'll let him go.

I cannot let that happen.

Whatever is inside Robyn's journal must hold vital information.

I need to get it from Luke's bedside drawer.

CHAPTER 3

I'm awake before the first ray of sunlight creeps through my curtains.

The clouds hang heavy over the still lagoon, pinks and purples swirling through the morning sky.

I splash cold water onto my face, attempting to ease my bloodshot eyes.

Last night I stared up at the ceiling for hours, feeling the tender parts of me that had been invaded by Luke.

I think of him now, lying in his gigantic four-poster bed... my sisters journal tucked away right next to him.

He has to know what happened to her. Why else would he be keeping it?

A hadeda ibis bird penetrates the silence with a guttural squawk.

River bolts to the window to chase it away.

As I finish my coffee I think about what I have to do. How I have to be around Luke.

I need him to invite me back to his place so I can get that book. If that means pretending to want him, so be it.

Robyn needs me.

After shovelling some avocado on toast into my mouth I take the short walk to the school, trailing through the graveyard. My brogues crush fallen protea petals scattered from the howling gale as I wind my way around the tombstones.

There's a dank smell all around me, filling my nostrils.

I wrap my coat tightly around me as I hurry on, eager to get away from the stench of death and decay.

I'm somewhat relieved when I make it to the school gates.

There's more people milling around the campus than usual and as I get closer, I notice camera crew amongst the crowd.

My heart plummets, heralding bad news.

Not another one, I hope.

My jaw is clenched.

One of my ballet students, Chloe, darts over to me, forgetting her usual poise.

There are tears in her eyes.

"Ms. Brady, I'm so glad you're here!"

"What's happened?" I ask, looking around for some sort of clue.

"Ms. Evans, I'm afraid I'm going to have to ask you to come with us," a police officer addresses Chloe.

She doesn't let go of my hands as she bursts into tears.

I'm stunned silent.

"Your parents will meet us at the station," the officer tells her.

"What's going on here?" I demand, feeling suddenly protective of my student.

Hungry eyes are all around us, wanting the same answers that I do.

"Ms. Evans was attacked in the school parking lot this morning."

It is only now that I notice the scratches and red marks on Chloe's neck.

The buttons on her school shirt have been ripped off.

"We have reason to believe this is related to the disappearances that have taken place lately."

My stomach drops.

Chloe cowers away from the police, wrapping her arms around herself.

Everything is spinning; the world goes quiet... until my eyes land on him. Luke. Strolling casually up to a group of students, his hands jammed into the pockets of his jeans, heedless of the chaos going on all around him.

When the frenzy of the local media abates, the headmaster calls the entire school faculty and the students to the hall.

I'm perched on a stool beside Cody, listening to the murmur of everyone filling the room.

I catch snippets of conversations. Some girls are accusing Chloe of lying.

"She's such an attention whore," one girls snarls and a handful of others seem to agree.

Some aren't so sure.

"That's another dancer targeted. Something is definitely going on!"

The names of all the missing girls are mentioned. Robyn's name is among them.

Theories and rumours are spread.

Cody shakes his head at me, a grim expression on his face.

The other teachers chat amongst themselves, none of them looking at me. They've all kept their distance from me since day one.

Cody's the only one who has made the effort. I look down at the watch on his wrist and stare at the hand tick, tick, tick.

"Quiet please," the headmaster booms as he enters the room.

Everyone shuffles in their seats, stopping mid sentence.

The only sound now is the heavy breathing from everyone waiting on tenterhooks.

Over two hundred pairs of eyes are on the headmaster and teachers.

I can feel their eyes piercing into the back of my neck.

"As I'm sure you're all aware, Chloe Evans was attacked this morning as she arrived in the school parking lot. As she was getting her backpack from the back-seat someone came up behind her and tried to drag her behind the bleachers. She did not get a good look at whoever did this, she said it happened too fast. Her injuries are not serious but she is, understandably, traumatized. Five young ladies have already fallen victim to someone unknown to us. Robyn Brady," the principal takes a moment to look down at me. I flush, not knowing where to look or how to respond. Cody rubs my shoulder softly.

"Angela Thompson, Corrie Turner, Susan Butterworth and most recently, Jessica Nicholls. Their whereabouts is still under investigation. We cannot lose hope. I can assure you that the police are working tirelessly to find them and the perpetrator behind this. We know these disappearances are all linked. Whoever is doing this seems to be targeting -," he pauses to clear his throat.

"Dancers."

The murmurs start up again. Everyone glances over to the remaining ballet students who are practically quivering with fear.

"However," he shouts over the frenzied whispers.

"I urge you *all* to take the utmost care both on and off campus. Walk in pairs. Do not isolate yourself. Be vigilant and look out for one another. While we want things to continue on as normally as possible, until this situation has been put to rest certain measures need to be put into place.

The local security company is here to teach you a bit more about safety. I ask you to give these men your undivided attention. I will not allow another student to go missing on my watch. Thank you."

He exits and allows a group of men kitted out in bullet proof vests, wielding batons and handguns to take over.

I twist in my seat, noticing how the usually glazed eyes of the students are wide open with focus. All except for Luke. He's crouched over in his seat, his phone illuminating an amused smile on his face.

By the end of the day five of my students have quit their roles in our upcoming ballet production, Giselle. We no longer have enough dancers to make this show work.

I can't say I blame them. Their ghostly maiden costumes hang limply from hooks in the dressing room. There is no one dancing to the sweet, ethereal sounds of Adolphe Adam's symphony.

My only hope is that Chloe will come back and take up her role as the peasant girl who falls for a deceitful nobleman, Albrecht, ever so coincidentally played by Luke.

Albrecht causes Giselle to die from a broken heart when she discovers he's betrothed to someone else, despite his seducing her.

It is in the second act that I have lost my dancers.

They were the Wilis, the spirits of maidens who had all died after having their hearts broken. I shiver as I realise how prevalent this story is.

No wonder the girls don't want to dance as ghosts, let alone dance at all.

As the story of Giselle goes on, the ghostly maidens summon Giselle from her grave through dance. They get their revenge on men by dancing them to death.

As the Wilis move on to target Giselle's lover, she saves him and herself from becoming one of them.

I swallow hard as Luke enters the hall, sword in hand.

There's no denying he looks devilishly handsome in his noble finery, leaning against our autumnal backdrop.

"Heard my sweet Giselle won't be in today. What should we do now?" he wiggles an eyebrow at me.

It's just the two of us, alone. I know what he's getting at.

My blood boils but I manage a seductive smile as I saunter over to him. I'm rolling the can of pepper-spray the security company had given to me around in my hand.

They'd donated a can to every student and staff member at the end of their chat with us.

My ruffled blouse has been left open enough to see my cleavage. His eyes fall there unapologetically.

"We can't keep doing this at school, Luke," I whisper into his ear. I let him watch me bite my lower lip.

He groans, rearranging himself in his tight leggings.

Steve, Giselle's hilarion, strides into the room, interrupting us. He's wearing a mottled fur costume and a vexing smirk on his face.

His role is the gamekeeper who is also in love with Giselle. He's suspicious of Albrecht and attempts to warn her but she doesn't listen.

He's still far enough away for me to be able to whisper, "your place after class..."

CHAPTER 4

Luke asks me to sit in the living-room when I get to his place.
For a moment I'm thrown off-guard. I'd expected us to head
straight to his bedroom.
I do as I'm told and nod when he offers me a drink.
I have to appear normal. Get him to trust me.
He sits beside me and traces his fingers along my knee. He's
sipping on what smells like neat whiskey.
Every part of me wants to shake him off of me but I allow his
fingers to creep up my leg.
"Piper, I need to say something," he looks at me with a
seriousness I'm not familiar with. He's usually so playful and
cheeky.
I blink up at him, eager to get this over and done with.
"I'm a little worried about you," he says.
I try to speak, to ask him what he means but he interrupts me.
"This isn't anything serious. You know that right?" he's wincing at
his words.
I almost scoff. The little shit thinks I'm falling for him!
I sit upright on the sofa, faltering.
"I've seen the way you look at me. Frankly I think it's becoming a
bit obvious to my friends. They keep talking about how you want
to... bang me. They can tell. If this is going to continue you really
need to be more discreet, babe."
The nerve of him! His fingers are venturing further north.
However baffled I am, I'm also momentarily humiliated.

The other students are talking about me this way!?
I'm flushed with embarrassment and want to curl into myself until I remember why I'm here. I've got to get that journal.
"Look, Luke-" I say, licking my freshly painted lips.
I force myself to smile at him.
"I definitely don't want this to stop! That's why I said we shouldn't do it at school any more. We both just need to be more careful, right?" I'm running my fingers through his hair, caressing the back of his neck. Goosebumps rise to the surface of his skin. I've got him.
He rests his head against my shoulder, pressing his lips to my collarbone.
The buttons on my blouse are quickly undone and my skirt pulled down to my ankles.
"These are nice," he slides his fingers into my pale blue underwear.
I try not to enjoy his touch as he begins rubbing me.
We aren't where we're supposed to be. I try to push him off of me and lead him into the bedroom but this only seems to excite him further.
"Want it rough, do you?" he grins at me, pushing me up against a wall so hard my feet leave the floor.
I take the opportunity, wrap my legs around his waist.
I fumble for his belt buckle, ripping it off once I've got a good grip. His jeans and briefs drop to the floor. I can feel him hardening, getting wet as he pokes his dick into my leg.
"Take me to your bed," I beg, but it's too late. In one swift thrust he's inside me, ramming me harder into the wall. I gasp in real pain, my nails embedded into his shoulders. I close my eyes and wait for it to end, the journal at the forefront of my mind.

He collapses on top of me once he's finished.
I fight the urge to squirm away from him.
Unlike the last time, Luke doesn't rush straight to the shower. He leans over me, his sweaty skin sticking to mine as he grabs our drinks.

"Bottoms up," he winks, draining his glass. I try and fail to smile as I toss whiskey down my throat in return.

"So Ms. Brady, is detention over?"

His eyes are sparkling mischievously but I can tell he wants me to leave.

I feel used.

How can I make him let me stay?

"Go shower. I'll get dressed so long," I mutter. Any flirtation in me has long gone.

He doesn't seem to notice the shift in my mood. Instead, he's tossing my clothes at me as he pulls his shirt over his head.

"Got somewhere to be. No time to shower. Besides, now I'll be able to smell you all over me for the rest of the day," he brings his fingers to his nose and breathes in deeply.

I want to throw up. The whiskey is churning in my stomach as my nausea levels rise.

I leave his house with barely a backwards glance.

I'm about to trudge back to my sisters cottage when I stop dead in my tracks.

Hiding behind the foliage of an Assegai tree, I wait for him to leave.

I slip a cigarette out of the packet in my handbag, light it up and suck in a deep lungful of smoke.

It doesn't take him long to come out and lock the front door behind him.

I watch him yet again bring his hand up to his nostrils and breathe me in. He smirks as he strolls down the road.

My lip curls up in disgust. As soon as he's around the bend I make the dash back to his house.

I don't bother with the front door, knowing it's locked. I circle the house in search of an open window. I'm surprised his windows don't have bars on them like the majority of the houses in the area, but it works in my favour when I find one slightly ajar by the kitchen.

I lift it up with some difficulty and hoist myself up onto the windowsill. I just manage to fit through it, knocking over a succulent that smashes all over the ceramic tiles.

"Fuck," I whisper, staring down at the mess. I stand dead still, listening closely for the sound of a security alarm. When I'm certain the place is disarmed, I quickly sweep up the broken pot and soil all over the floor. I'm shaking, wondering if he will notice it missing when he comes home.

I creep into his bedroom on wobbly legs.

My eyes land on his bedside drawer straight away.

As I'm walking towards it I notice his computer screen is on.

There are several tabs open. Facebook pages dedicated to each of the missing girls. My sister, Angela, Corrie, Susan, and Jessica. All of the pages are active, comments filtering in every few minutes. Thoughts, prayers, well wishes. I can see all of this on my own computer at the cottage, so I don't fiddle with it.

Open in another tab is a Google search for '*Traits of a sociopath.*' My brain rattles.

There's a notepad and pen by the mouse and I flip it open. He's written down some of the traits he's found.

Impulsive. Emotional yet shows no remorse or guilt for their actions. Psychopaths tend to be master manipulators.

He's underlined things like pathological lying, narcissism and a grandiose sense of their worth. At the bottom of the page he's jotted down a question.

Are psychopaths predominantly men or women???

There are three question-marks alongside it. I flick over to the next sheet of paper but there's nothing else written down, just a book of blank pages.

There's a video file open too, which I click on to. The sound of sex fills the room, coming from his speakers. It shocks me so much that I feel like my heart is going to explode.

With a shaky hand I mute the volume and look closely at the video.

Luke's recording himself having sex with someone.

I can't see her face. He's holding her ponytail like a handlebar, doing her from behind.

There's a tiny tattoo of a scorpion between the dimples on her lower-back. I don't know why I can't look away.

He drops her hair, letting it fall down her back in waves. Her ass is raw from his slaps.

He smacks her again and I can see her flinch but when she turns around to look at him, her eyes are smiling into the camera. She's enjoying it.

I know those eyes. I know that face.

It's Jessica's face.

One of the missing girls.

His desk has one drawer to the right which I open. I rummage through leaky pens, post-it notes and raw protein bars when my fingers find something right at the back. It feels like a soft wad of material.

I pull it out curiously to see a scrunched up pair of dirty panties.

I flick them away, wiping my hands in disgust. Whose are they!?

I feel the need to leave straight away but know I need to get my sisters journal first.

I clamber over to the drawer and dig inside for the book.

It's gone.

I empty the entire drawer just to make sure. I look under the bed and in the shoe boxes stacked in his wardrobe. I can't find it anywhere.

I'm shaking with frustration and adrenalin.

I'm in such a state I hardly hear the front door slamming closed from down the hallway.

There's no chance of me making it to the open window without him seeing me.

I frantically look around for a place to hide.

I'm cramming myself behind his bedroom door when I hear his voice.

"She's such a bore until it comes to sex. I mean, she's no where near as flexible as Robyn but she's a ton of fun alright!"

Someone laughs at what he's saying. I'm too petrified to be angry at the things he's saying about me and my sister right now, but I'm acutely aware of the fact that he was with her, too.

"I still have no idea how you manage to nail the teachers." It's Steve's voice.

"I'd share but I doubt she'd be into that," Luke cackles, cracking open a can of beer.

They cheers and get lost in conversation about the girls in school. Who they've been with, who they want to and who they never would. It's despicable.

I'm just starting to edge my way out of my hiding place when Luke announces he need to 'take a slash.'

He's already unzipping his pants as he walks through his bedroom door.

My heart thunders violently as he swings his door shut behind him, leaving me completely exposed. Luckily he doesn't turn around, he walks straight into the bathroom which gives me time to drop to my knees and crawl to a safer spot.

I can hear his piss hitting the water in the toilet bowl. I can hear him humming some sort of classical music.

I'm crouched behind the other side of his bed when he flushes the toilet and walks back into his room.

I hold my breath and listen to his footsteps, waiting for him to leave the room.

As he's almost out the door, he stops. I can see the leather tip of his boot tapping up and down. The house is silent.

He takes one step, then pauses again. I hear his knees crack as he bends down, close to his computer.

I see it then. The pair of panties I'd flicked out of my fingers. Luke scoops them up, still bent down low. I can hear him twisting his body left to right.

I've been holding my breath so long I'm turning blue. My lips silently mouthing the word, '*Please, please, please,*' over and over again.

"Jesus, Luke. What're you doing in there, taking a shit?" Steve calls. I take the chance to grab lungfuls of air.

"Someone's been in here..." Luke shouts back, crushing the panties into his fist and pocketing them. "Probably Ms. Brady, man?" Steve leans against the door frame.

"Someone's gone through my desk," Luke pushes himself up from his haunches and opens the drawer to investigate.
"Nosy bitch!" Steve laughs through a beer belch.
"Yeah... nosy bitch," he mutters, unconvinced.

*

A lone heron watches me curiously as I kick the lapping lagoon water on my way back home. Clouds roll past me, the African sky already painted pastel pink.
I bypass the graveyard today, taking the long way home along the waters edge.
I'm racking my brain, trying to think where my sisters journal could possibly be. I don't know Luke's place well enough.
I don't know if he has a safe or another storage facility somewhere.
Questions trickle through my head. Why would he move it? Whose underwear is he keeping in his drawer?
I'm so consumed with my thoughts that I'm startled when I find myself right outside the cottage. I don't really remember getting here.
There's more flowers and cards perched on the stoop, all for my sister.
I have no doubt the houses of the other missing girls are also flooded with things like this.
I sigh as I scoop up the bouquets and cards that I won't open, kick the door ajar and make my way inside.
I call out for River and wait for the scampering sound of her claws on the floorboards.
They don't come.
I drop my bag and poke my head into every room.
Sometimes she sneaks into the second bedroom and makes the bed her own, but today she's no where to be seen.
It's a feeling that hits me out of no where. Dread.
Rushing out into the overgrown garden, I call her name frantically.

I'm fighting back tears that sting at my eyes.

I call her name once more, as loudly as I possibly can and fall silent.

The echo of my voice travels around me. The only other thing I can hear is the rumble of cars as they pass by the cottage and the rustling of trees in the breeze.

I stay silent, listening intently.

The sound of something scratching against wood comes from my left.

I follow, finding my way around the back of my sisters place.

There's a tiny shed covered in bird-shit at the corner of the property. The windows are smashed and there's something nailed to the door.

I approach it hesitantly, the sound of scratching getting louder.

I tear the note from a rusted nail that's been jammed into the wood.

'Stop searching.'

The words are scribbled roughly, angrily.

My breathing quickens as I pocket the note and tug at the door.

"River!?" I scream desperately.

There's a dull whine coming from inside.

I yank the door open and River limps up to me. I'm almost certain I'm going to throw up as I drop to the floor.

Her leg has been completely sawed off.

CHAPTER 5

It was a warning.

I'm curled in bed by myself while River has to stay at the veterinary clinic after surgery.

It's so quiet without the sound of her soft snores at my feet at night.

I've opened a case but once again I know the police won't do anything more than they already have.

They fingerprinted everything. Found nothing. The level of competency here isn't much.

I'm not used to being without River.

I look at the note again. It's the one thing I didn't tell the police about.

The writing looks abnormally shaky, like it had been written by a child.

My stomach growls hungrily but I don't want to eat. I keep thinking of River, alone in a cage in the clinic. One beautiful leg gone.

I'm devastated.

I squeeze my knees and feel a sense of loneliness wash over me. Unwelcome memories of Michael creep up on me. The sensation of his arms around me, the kisses on my forehead.

Even after what he's done I'd do anything to feel that sense of love right now.

I unlock my phone with my thumbprint and scroll through our last messages. The goodbyes.

I'm still amazed at how he could just let me go, forget about me like I was never there at all.

I want to message him – tell him about River. He'd given her to me last Valentine's Day. It's hard to believe that was less than a year ago.

River had popped her tiny black and white head out of a pink box and blinked up at me with topaz eyes. I loved her instantly and everything she symbolised.

She was the start of our future – our family.

Around her collar hung a sparkling diamond ring. It was a tiny bit too big for me but it was everything I'd ever wanted in a ring. He'd listened well.

After that I'd spend my afternoons in the dog park, letting River play and interact with the other dogs while I planned our wedding.

I'd been so lucky having someone like Michael who refused to let me work.

He wanted me to spend my days being creative, enjoying my hobbies.

He'd told me he earned enough to support us both. He'd said his hours were flexible and he wanted me to be available if he fancied taking off somewhere at the spur of the moment.

I must admit I enjoyed the idea at first, especially when I was consumed with the wedding plans. Michael would get home around dinner time and listen to me gush about different venues I'd discovered and my shock at how astronomical the prices of caterers were.

My bridesmaids started coming over every Tuesday evening to help.

We'd crack open a few bottles of wine, watch hilarious YouTube videos of wedding speeches.

We'd peruse bridal magazines, cut things out and slap them onto the mood board we'd created.

We'd planned it so that River would be a part of the day. We got quotes from various dog trainers so that River could learn to carry the rings down the aisle. She'd been the one who had given me the engagement ring, after all.

As cliché as it all sounded, it was my dream come true.

I never expected Michael to do what he did.

It was my maid of honour, Beatrix, who told me.

Michael couldn't do it himself.

He'd gotten her pregnant – and they were keeping the baby.

I left as soon as I found out, River right at my heels.

I'd thanked God for the savings I'd kept away from my time on the yachts. I'd planned on using the savings to help pay for our wedding but relief had flooded through me as I realised what a waste those deposits would have been.

I sigh, hating myself for wanting Michael right now.

Deep down, I know he doesn't deserve me but the need to be loved and protected is overwhelming.

I shut my phone down before I have the chance to send Michael a message I know I'll regret.

Last I heard, my maid of honour had hosted a gender reveal party at a shooting range. I couldn't believe it had come around so soon. Where had time gone?

Both her and Michael had shot glocks at black balloons which had sprayed pink confetti everywhere.

Of course I'd sneaked onto social media to see the photographs. I'm a huge fan of torturing myself, it seems.

There was a picture of the two of them grinning at the camera surrounded by a sea of pink. The photo is captioned, *'We can't wait to meet our baby girl, Shiloh!'*

I flinched when I read it.

I was surprised by how many people who knew me, who were *friends* with me, clicked 'like' on the photo.

It had been *me* and Michael who had been together for six years! *Me* and Michael who had sent our wedding invitations out to all the people 'liking' this photograph. They all knew he'd cheated! They'd cheated... yet they still liked this photo.

There were over one hundred and sixty comments with congratulations and well wishes. I'd been forgotten by everyone.

I wanted to see comments bad mouthing them for what they'd

done to me.

I wanted people to tell them shooting while pregnant was a stupid thing to do.

I mean, not only is the sound deafening but there was the possibility of lead poisoning too.

As someone who has had multiple miscarriages I'd bristled at the thought of what could happen at a shooting range.

The membrane could rupture or the foetal development could be compromised.

I know I shouldn't care, but I do.

Beatrix had been my best friend since pre-school.

I'd never wish losing a child on anyone. Not even her.

What I hate is that Michael would actually *care* if he lost a child this time. She had been able to give him the one thing that I never could. Fatherhood.

I wonder if he ever thinks of me. Of the life he used to have before leaving me for my best friend.

I wonder how long they'd been seeing each other behind my back and if he'd still be with me if he hadn't gotten her pregnant. Would I want him to be? If the wool had been pulled over my eyes would I want him back in my life?

I toss my phone to the empty side of my bed and pad into the kitchen.

I rip a packet of seasoning open while the kettle boils and sprinkle it over my pot of noodles.

I'd been so looking forward to pay day to stock up on real food again – but now it seems I'll need to take a loan from the bank to pay for River's vet bills.

*

The next morning more press conferences are held by the families of the missing girls.

I have to make a speech for Robyn.

I beg for her safe return.

I say I feel her with me every second of every day... but the truth is I haven't felt my sisters presence for quite some time.

CHAPTER 6

Jesus, Piper is so predictable.

I can't stand seeing her large green eyes well up as she looks at the camera. The way her voice cracks and her slender little fingers tremble as they clutch onto the podium.

All the speeches the families give for their precious girls are so monotonous.

"Please bring our darling daughter home to us-" yada, yada, yada.

Those little sluts will never be coming back, don't they see that yet?

After I've had my fun with them I'll tear them to pieces one by one.

I suppose I'm a little bit like Jack the Ripper, aren't I? Killing off all the whores.

I always did love his work.

Perhaps I should write the police a letter, just like he did! The thought is exciting, but I know times have changed. They'd be able to pick up DNA and too many clues if I did that... and I'm having far too much fun for that to happen.

I clutch the hood around my neck as the ferocity of the wind picks up. I'm not supposed to be here, but there's something so satisfying about seeing these families and the students suffer.

I wasn't planning on Piper discovering the journal. At first it had

made me want to punch my fist through a wall but then I realised it could possibly work in my favour.
If I play my cards right, that is.

I set off for the outskirts of town. To the rural, fabulously isolated industrial area where I've been spending most of my time lately. It couldn't be a more perfect, nondescript location. Hundreds of abandoned, partly burnt down buildings to choose from. It's a place long since forgotten about, the best bit being that no one is around... so no one can hear the screams.

I try to keep them all gagged and bound but sometimes the ones that still have the energy manage to chew through the tape I've slapped around their pretty little mouths.
I stop at a tiny shop selling the basics and load up on food.
Everything I put into the basket is as fattening as I can find.
It was delightful to watch how repulsed the girls were by their meals at first.
They'd refused to eat.
Didn't want to harm their sculpted ballerina figures. But now? They're ravenous!
I can physically see them plumping up right before my eyes.
They're dirty. The flawless make-up, the hair-sprayed up-dos, the intensely sweet scent of their perfumes have melted away with sweat and muck.
They have become the grimy, disgusting whores I know they really are.
Next time their families see them, in the morgue, they'll hardly be able to identify them.
The images seared into their heads of their perfect, beautiful daughters' will forever be replaced with the filth they became before they were murdered.
I haven't quite gotten around to thinking how I'm going to do it. If I can even do it.
All I know is that my anger is so intense, I can't imagine it being a problem.

They deserve to die for what they've done.
I wish I could be there to see the looks on their parents faces... the
confusion.
Maybe they'll look at their daughters' with that lip-curling
repulsion the girls had when I tossed them greasy fries and lumps
of fat cut from steak for the first time.
Some still cry as they put the cooked animal fat to their lips. They
grimace as they gnaw with their teeth that have started turning a
fantastic shade of yellow.
Others have lost all sense of their elegance already. They devour
everything they're given like the greedy, selfish pigs they've
always been.

I think about my next victim. Chloe is going to be on high alert
after her narrow escape.
Fucking bitch.
I'm not even sure if she's going to come back to the school.
She hasn't left her house since she got away from me.
I see her sometimes, peering out from behind her curtains when I
walk past her house – but I have no idea when she's planning on
going back to school or anything.

There's an atrocious stench coming from the basement. A
combination of piss, shit and unwashed bodies.
The blood from their cycles mottled and dried into their pants.
Anton Chekhov, a Russian short story writer, one of my favorites,
once said, 'I don't understand anything about the ballet; all I
know is that during the intervals the ballerinas stink like horses.'
Oh, Chekhov, they stink far worse than that right now.

I wonder if I should play with them today.
I do that sometimes. Put on a voice, pretend to be someone
coming to their rescue.
I love hearing their moans get louder from behind their taped
mouths.
I start to hear the scraping and toppling over of chairs as they

each try to make enough noise for their saviour to hear them.
I'm not in a very playful mood today, though. Not after seeing
Piper.
She's going to have to be taken care of now, too.
That was never the plan. I don't want to harm her, but she's done
it to herself now.
She is just like the rest of them.
I hadn't necessarily wanted to hurt her stupid dog either but I'd
needed a leg up (ha!).
Every time I came near that dog she'd start growling at me.
I couldn't have her raising suspicion or causing a scene. With her
gone for a few days Piper is alone. Vulnerable.
An easy target.
Even if that dog comes home before I have a chance to get Piper,
I could outrun her now.
She'll be weak, slower – useless really.
I opted not to kill the mangy mutt because it's not the dogs fault
and I'm not a bad person.
I just want justice against those who have done me and my
relationship wrong.

CHAPTER 7

My heart shatters at the sight of River who, regardless of her operation, has huge eyes and a wagging tail as soon as she sees me. It fills me with equal amounts of sadness and love.
I don't give a shit what that note says, I'm going to find out who did this to her.

Ushering her into the cottage, River slumps down on her bed.
She's already exhausted from limping from the car.
I'm so used to her bounding around full of energy and excitement that it's hard to think of her as the same dog.
The vet assured me that she'll adapt quickly to three legs, but I still have no idea how to deal with it.
I have no clue how she'll cope on our usual walks initially. I just hope I'm going to do a good enough job looking after her.
There's a card from the vet with a short poem inside of it that I perch up on the fireplace mantle.
It's just a cheap print out from the internet that they've folded themselves, but it's the thought that counts. It's enough to make me cry.
I do just that, curling up in River's dog bed with her and sobbing into her fur. I stay with her for a few hours while the fire crackles away.
We're both exhausted and happy to have each other close.
This isn't like me. I used to be the strong one, but I can't handle it anymore.
I feel so overwhelmed.

I miss Robyn. I'm hurting for River. I'm scared of whoever is out there, abducting these girls.
Could it really be Luke? Are the girls alive? Is Robyn out there? As these questions fill my mind, I breathe in my dogs new, medicinal smell.

I'm hoping Robyn's alarm system is adequate protection. I've left River in a room where there are no sensors but the windows are barred.
I've put my phone on loud so if the security company calls me and tells me there's been a break-in I can get right back within minutes.
I give her a kiss on the snout and tell her I'll be back soon.
She whimpers softly as I leave, licking sorely at her bandages.

*

There's a car I'm not familiar with parked outside Luke's house.
I planned on visiting him but if someone else is there they'll wonder right away why a teacher is visiting a student after hours.
I send him a message instead, telling him I *'need'* him with a fire emoji.
It revolts me to press send.
My only way back into his house safely is to flirt and have him invite me over – if he'll even do that after the other day.
I feel like I've mucked things up already.
While I wait for his reply, I head down to the local pub.
My emotions are all over the place after picking up River so I really just need a drink to calm down.

The pub is like a cavern, giving the illusion that it's already late at night. It makes my insecurities of day drinking mellow.
I order a vodka tonic and squeeze a slice of lime over it.
I really should be used to sitting alone in silence by now, but all I want to do is wrap my arms around myself and scream.
I guess the background noise from the other drinkers helps.

There's more people here than I expected, considering the time. I wonder if it's the disappearances of all the girls that's luring people into the pub before five-o'clock.

I down the drink surprisingly fast and order another, already feeling looser limbed. A little tingly.

There's a live band setting up in the corner, tuning their guitars and adjusting the sound.

After the second drink everything starts feeling a bit like a dream.

There isn't one person in the pub not talking about the girls. Potential suspects. Motives. Rumours are running wild.

If you trawl through Facebook or Google you can get the stories of how the girls all disappeared.

Corrie disappeared while she was on her way to buy a carton of milk for her mother. Nothing was picked up on CCTV footage.

Angela was walking home after a babysitting job. Ostensibly, the parents had drank too much wine to give her a lift home.

Jessica had sent her father a text message letting him know that she'd be home late from a date. She'd never told him who she was out with and no one had come forward to say it was them. There were also just a handful of restaurants in town and none of them had served Jessica that night.

Was the text really sent from her?

Susan lived in her own garden flat on the same property as her parents. Her bed was unmade and there was a full cup of coffee now growing mouldy on her bedside table.

From the look of it, she'd been ready for bed when she disappeared.

Perhaps someone had knocked on her door. Maybe she'd thought it was her parents. Yet, there wasn't even a sign of a struggle.

Then there's Robyn.

No one quite knows when she disappeared. They can't give me a date or a time.

Everyone has their own theory about what's going on.

All any of us have are kernels of information. There's nothing to go on, really.

I have no one to share my own theory with. If I tell someone I suspect Luke, they'll want to know why.

I guess it's a good thing I don't have anyone to tell.

The band starts up, beginning with a cover from Mumford & Sons.

It's a song I've always loved, from the album, Babel.

It feels like I'm listening to the lyrics for the very first time. I'm relating to every word. The woozy eyes, the weakness I need to show. My heart stumbling on things I don't know. Struggling to find any truth in the lies.

In this moment, it feels like the song was written for me.

When the singer flips back his unruly hair and sings, *'Lend me your heart and I'll just let you fall,'* I want to cry.

It reminds me of Michael. Of what he did.

Maybe it's not what the song means, but it's how I'm interpreting it.

Maybe the song means something entirely different.

I feel tipsy. The back of my head is heating up.

There's a dull buzzing in my ears.

I can feel myself swaying on the barstool.

I'm not used to drinking much, it doesn't mix well with my medication. It makes me very sleepy.

I've always been cautious about drinking anyway.

Robyn and I were in the foster system from the day we were born because of alcoholic birth parents.

We had Fetal Alcohol Syndrome. We struggled all throughout our childhoods with sleeping problems and behavioural issues.

We were always much smaller than our classmates and before puberty the way people teased us was relentless.

I guess we're just lucky we got to stay together throughout all of the foster homes. We got through it together.

Sometimes I wonder what it would be like today had we been separated.

I know alcoholism is hereditary. I know we are at greater risk of liking a drink a bit too much, but right now I can't think of another way to get through the day.

The next song starts. Harmonica opening a Bob Dylan song.

The band's right in the middle of the song when the door to the pub blows open.

I can just make out two people heading down the concrete steps and ordering drinks from the bar.

It's only as they walk by me that I realise who they are.

Luke and Bibiana.

My heart sky rockets with both fear and the shock of seeing him here.

He has my sisters journal. He has my sisters journal. *He has my sisters journal.*

I can't think of anything else. It's hard to contain myself after a couple of drinks, to not just go right up to him and tell him I know he has it.

He's holding the small of Bibiana's back, guiding her to a table.

It makes me think of that sex tape. Of the tattoo on Jessica's back.

Is Bibiana next?

His eyes flick over me with surprise.

"Ms. Brady," he nods, like he barely knows me.

I know he has to be this way. Treat me like a student would treat their teacher. Nothing more.

I wonder if he's seen the message I sent him earlier. I feel embarrassed having sent it now.

I swallow hard and nod back at the two of them.

Bibiana smiles sweetly at me and as they walk past I hear her giggle, whispering something into his ear.

He laughs back at whatever she's said, smacking her lightly on the bum.

My mind races, remembering the slap marks swelling up on Jessica's backside in that video.

They look over at me as they talk animatedly.

They must find it awkward to be sitting in the same pub as their teacher.

I can't quite explain the feeling that rolls through me.

It can't be jealousy, surely.

Suddenly I feel ashamed that I have a drink in my hand.

Caught in the act.

My mind is spinning. I'm over-thinking everything.

Paranoia washes over me as I wonder what they are saying about me.

I haven't taken my pills today.

I need to take my pills.

I twist a lock of greying hair around my finger, trying not to look at them.

Luke's positioned them at a table right in my line of sight.

He must have done it purposefully.

He's toying with me.

Bibiana twirls a finger through her ponytail. Her handlebar.

I can feel my pulse thumping in my neck. The pub is getting hotter.

The back of my neck is wet from sweat.

I try to calm myself. I can't have a panic attack here. Not now.

Not in front of them.

Biabana is leaning over the table towards him, chatting over the music.

I catch sight of myself in a Bell's Whiskey mirror, like a deer in the headlights.

My eyes are huge, bewildered.

When the band leaves the stage I give a tepid clap and gather my things to leave.

I'm on my way out the door when Cody bumps into me.

"Looks like we both have the same idea," he smiles, ordering a gin from the barman.

I really don't want to be alone right now, so I decide to stay.

It's the only time I see Luke glance over at me, realising I'm not alone any more.

Two can play at this game.

I don't even know why I want to make him jealous.

I tell Cody about what happened to River. It's so hard to talk about it.

It's then I realise I haven't spoken to anyone about it apart from the vet and police. I haven't spoken to anyone about anything in a while.

He's a good listener. He's quiet and never breaks eye contact.

It's exactly what I've been needing.

After our last two meetings I'm starting to feel at ease around him, despite his obvious attraction towards me... and my sister.

He makes it easy to loosen up. Open up.

I order drink after drink, spilling out all of my emotions.

I just don't care right now.

Out of the corner of my eye I can see Bibiana's hands in Luke's.

His thumb is stroking her wrist and he's giving her his smile he knows charms the strongest of women.

It makes me want to vomit.

I lose count in how many drinks I have, but when I try to go to the bathroom I topple off the barstool.

Cody catches me quickly, steadying me with a strong arm.

I can feel so many eyes on me.

Luke and Bibiana twist in their seats to watch me.

Bibiana covers her mouth, muffling her laughter. I see Luke shake his head, comment something and look away from me.

I'm embarrassed and want to go home.

I need to take my pills.

Cody helps me up the steps and puts me into his car.

The smell of the leather seats is overpowering.

I roll the window down, gulping down the fresh air as his car creeps along the main road.

"I know it can't be easy for you with Robyn being gone," he's saying. His words float through me.

I nod and shake my head at the same time, not sure which one to do. Yes, it's hard. No, it's not easy.

"I'm here if you ever need to talk."

He pulls up outside of the cottage.

I have a sudden wave of nausea. He sits me down on the pavement and tells me to breathe in deeply.

He's stroking my back and brushing my hair from my face. His touch is soothing. Confusing.

"Shouldn't have had so much to drink," I hiccup.

"We all need an outlet every so often," he says.

"I miss her," I admit, starting to cry.

Tears stream down my cheeks and land onto his shoulders when he pulls me in for a hug.

He doesn't say anything.

He doesn't tell me it's all going to be OK. He can't. He doesn't know that.

Instead he holds me tightly.

"We all miss her," he sighs.

When I've somewhat collected myself Cody walks me to the front door. I'm gripping his forearm to balance myself.

It feels like I'm walking on clouds.

He's not an attractive man, but I look up at him with gratefulness. The world spins.

I don't see it coming when I wrap my arms around his neck and kiss him drunkenly on the lips.

He's rigid for a moment, unsure of what to do but soon he eases up.

He melts into my lips, his hands snaking around my waist.

I'm up against the door, his musty scent rubbing onto my skin.

He feels good.

For just a moment, I close my eyes and pretend it's Michael, that I'm back in his arms and kissing him again.

I snap back into reality when he lets out a slight moan.

I start laughing, pulling away from him.

"Thank you for looking after me," I slur through giggles.

He looks so taken-aback and struggles to find his voice.

I close the door on him after a small smile.

What the fuck did I just do?

*

I check on River once I'm back inside, still feeling Cody's wet lips against mine.

Her bandages are seeping but she's fast asleep, snoring softly, so I leave her sleeping in the kitchen.

I drunkenly kick off my shoes and fall into bed, still fully dressed. Being in the room without River feels cold and lonely.

I touch the empty side of the bed, thinking back to when I shared it with Michael... with anyone, really.

It hits me just how alone I am now.

I clamp my eyes tightly shut and let out a sigh.

"Goodnight River..." I whisper, curling over onto my side.

"Goodnight... Piper," someone's voice coming from everywhere and no where all at once fills the room.

I jump up in a blind panic.

"What the fuck!?" I bellow, flying from the bed and slapping my hand down on the light switch across the room.

I look around wildly. There's no one here.

Confused, I rip open the bedroom door and look around. I'm riddled with nerves.

The house is silent. I am alone.

Am I going mad?

The voice was loud enough for me to still make out every word spoken, loud and clear. This unfamiliar voice is echoing in my head.

It was real. It had to be!

"Hello?" I call out, gripping the door for support.

I wait anxiously for a response.

Nothing.

Tears roll down my cheeks.

What is happening to me?

I think about messaging Cody and asking him to come back.

I don't want to be alone any more.

Walking slowly back across the room, I pick up my phone and start punching in his number but stop myself.

I'm not ready.

I can't fall back into old patterns.

I need to get over Michael.

Alone.

I get back into bed and wrap the blankets around me, leaving the main light on.

I let out a tiny laugh. The irony.

I'm afraid of the dark.

It's like I'm nine years old all over again.

I close my eyes, starting to let sleep envelope me when suddenly the voice reverberates throughout the room again.

This time it isn't words, but a chuckle I hear.

My eyes grow huge in terror.

This time I know that it was real. I wasn't imagining it.

I'm petrified something is under the bed. What if they grab my ankles if I try to run out of the room?

I need River in here to protect me, but right now I need to protect her.

What if someone has come back to finish off the job with her?

I dial the number for the police and hurtle out of the room, bracing myself for an attack that doesn't come.

"Don't forget what I told you, Piper. Stop. Searching!"

It's a voice I've never heard before. It doesn't sound real.

It sounds distorted. Fake. Menacing.

"Please. Please help me. There's someone in my house!" I scream over the voice all around me when the woman on the other end of the line picks up.

Hurriedly, I try my best to get River up and out of the house.

Despite the pain she's in she knows that something is wrong and starts barking frantically.

I give the woman my sisters address and huddle into River on the side-walk, shivering and shaking in the cold night.

Every rustle in the bushes frightens me senseless as I wait.

It feels like the sirens take hours to come blaring up the driveway, but it must have only been a couple of minutes.

Two big, sturdy officers equipped with handguns shake my hand in turn.

Detective Engelbrecht and Officer Jensen.

One of them is the one who came to my house to fingerprint

things when I'd found River in the shed.

He eyes me warily.

I tell them the story, my words slightly slurred.

Detective Engelbrecht stays with me on the side-walk when I beg not to be left alone, Officer Jensen heads inside to investigate.

"How much have you had to drink tonight Ms. Brady?" Engelbrecht asks me.

His question feels invasive. Judgemental.

"Not enough," I hiccup, instantly regretting my lame attempt at a joke. He shoots me a dirty look.

"Look, I know what I heard. There was someone inside that house!"

River is panting, her eyes darting around in distress.

"Ms. Brady, I hope you don't mind me offering you a bit of advice. I know you've been through something quite traumatic with your dog – but try lay off the booze. It doesn't help much. Trust me, I know!" he chuckles, slapping his belly heartily.

"But it *could* have been whoever did this to her coming back to do more, couldn't it?!" I gesture desperately at River, needing them to understand me.

I'm not crazy, I want to say.

He shrugs his bulky shoulders and we sit in silence while we wait for Jensen to reappear. When he does, he asks us to follow him back inside.

"Did you say this was your sister's place, ma'am?" he asks me, his arms folded.

I nod quickly.

"Were you aware that she has Alexa Echo with dots in every room in the place?" his eyebrow cocks up.

He's looking at me like I'm an idiot.

I frown, shaking my head dumbly.

I've never been one for all this modern technology. I've never even heard of Alexa Echo.

Michael used to always talk to our television and say, 'OK Google," and I always thought it was bizarre.

He sighs, leading me to the bedroom and producing a small grey speaker I've never noticed before.

I look at it, puzzled.

"It seems that the broadcasting setting was on tonight," he speaks slowly, as though talking to a child.

I don't know if it's because he thinks I'm stupid or just drunk.

I can smell the alcohol on myself, so I assume the latter.

"I'm sorry, I don't understand what you're saying?" I say.

"Your Bluetooth must have been switched on. My guess is a neighbour hacked into the system and tried to prank you."

There's a slight smirk on his lips.

He thinks this is funny.

I close my eyes, trying to process what he's saying.

I want to tell them about what was actually said.

About the note I found pinned to the shed. The warning to stop searching. Hearing those words spoken out loud tonight.

It has to be whoever did this to my dog.

I am not safe! I want to scream it at them; but I can't.

I stop myself and swallow my words.

Instead, I steady myself and whisper, "so, what do I do now?"

I'm scared.

"I'll deactivate all of the dots throughout the house. The only other thing I can suggest is encrypting your WiFi. It makes it trickier to hack," he winks.

"But the voice – it didn't sound real! It was like some sort of voice modulator. Is it not illegal for someone to hack in anyway?! Isn't there something else you can do?"

I'm rambling now, panic rising knowing that they're about to leave me alone again.

"I've looked in every room and every nook and cranny. There's no one here, Piper. Get some sleep now."

I feel useless as I walk them to the front door after they've deactivated the dots.

I don't know what to do.

They clamber back into their police car and as they drive away I can see them shaking their heads at one another.

I don't want to go back inside but I have no choice.

I race into the bedroom, grabbing the speaker and storm out to chuck it in the bin outside.

No matter how hard I try, it's impossible to get to sleep and I'm too scared to take sleeping tablets.

I am instantly sobered and on high alert until the sun starts to rise.

CHAPTER 8

On Sunday I hide under my blankets with River, nursing my
hangover with a turmeric root tea, watching Criminal Minds.
I'm trying to distract myself.
There's been no more voices coming to me but I'm so shaken up
and still can't sleep.
How far is this person going to go to scare me? I wish the police
had done more.
My throat feels raw from alcohol, smoke and screaming.
I'm thankful I don't need to leave the cottage today. Too scared to
face the world.
My memory from last night is foggy but I remember what I did.
I remember the look on Cody's face.
I remember how surprisingly soft his lips were. Not like the
hardness and eagerness of Luke's kisses.
It was only a few seconds, if that, but it changed everything.
I'm not attracted to him at all but I like the way he makes me feel.
Listened to. Safe. Protected. Valued.
I find myself wanting to tell him about Luke and about the voice
from last night. I want to tell him the truth about River.
At the bar I'd told him she'd been run over and had to get her leg
amputated. My collection of lies and secrets just keeps growing. I
don't know if I can keep up with all of them anymore.
Maybe Cody could help me. Maybe he'll know what to do.
I rub my temple, knowing it's a bad idea.
He's sent me two text messages. One last night after he left,

thanking me for the evening.

Wow. That was... unexpected. Thank you for tonight. I hope you don't feel too bad tomorrow. C.

I hadn't replied.
I don't even recall opening his message last night.
There had been too much adrenalin coursing through my body after the cops had left – I just saw it this morning when I woke up face down in bed, drooling onto my pillow.
He messaged again an hour ago, asking me how I am.

Hope you slept well! Can I bring you anything? Coffee, croissant, some pain meds? C.

I don't know what to say to him. I feel suffocated.
This is unexpected.

His eagerness pushes me away. I'm not used to it.
In my past relationship I always had to work so hard for attention.
I had never known what Michael was thinking or feeling.
It had eaten away at me like a cancer and I'd festered with it, always over-thinking every little thing.
'What are you thinking?'
'How are you feeling?'
Those were questions I'd found myself asking him more times in a day than I could count in an attempt to fill up the silence between us.
The evening we got back from the hospital after I'd pushed our dead baby out, neither of us had words.
Now that I think about it, perhaps that's where the silence began.
The uncertainty.
Then the second time, it never even got to a stage of needing to push the baby out of my system.
It was too early for that.
I'd gone in to see the doctor with pain in my pelvis.

I'd thought he'd tell me I just needed bed rest. Tell me to take it easy. Relax. Keep my baby safe.

I never imagined I'd leave knowing that there was no possible way to save our baby.

'It will come out in it's own time,' the doctor had told us as he'd explained how it had started to grow in the fallopian tubes.

He'd called it a 'tubal pregnancy.'

I didn't understand my body, it's unwillingness to let me have a child.

I was so angry and alone – and that's when the depression had flared up again.

I had to go through it all alone. I had to see what would have been my child seeping onto sanitary pads and sliding down into the toilet bowl every time I went to the bathroom.

It was never far enough along to find out the sex, but I'd always wondered.

I'd envision myself with a boy and a girl, in the end. Two perfect, healthy little human beings.

Michael would be pushing them on swings, their sweet chortles filling up our home as I planted kisses on their little button noses.

I imagined taking them for walks with River attached to the pram, laying out a picnic blanket by the creek and watching them discovering the world.

It's what I've wanted for so long but after Michael broke up with me I told myself I would never have that.

How could I, with anyone else other than him?

Cody is pandering to my every need after just one kiss and I wish I could accept it but I can't stand it.

He's too much too soon.

I want to wipe every trace of him from my lips and mind.

I start to type him a message back, just to be polite.

All good. See you in class. P.

I hit send, knowing how deflated he will be when he reads my message but I have too many other things on my mind to worry about that.

My heart aches. Deep down all I want is to be loved and looked after, to be happy.

Why do I always push people away?

I've pushed away all my other bridesmaids.

It's not like they haven't tried to reach out.

I pushed away Beatrix and Michael when they tried to tell me how sorry they were.

I've pushed away Cody who really only wants to help.

I even pushed Robyn away. I didn't open up to her and tell her about what happened.

Why do I do this?

For so many years I was happy to explore the world, be alone.

Then I met Michael and I got a taste for what life would be like with someone by my side. It was all-consuming. Addictive.

It was cut short. When that dream was ripped away from me, I lost it.

I've become so desperate to find my place in the world but I'm too scared to actually accept it when it comes close now.

Every time I open up Facebook I see people's lives moving forward when mine is standing still.

I see old school friends announcing their pregnancies and job promotions.

I see couples getting engaged, married, buying their first house.

It makes me feel angry. At them. At me. At life.

When did it all get like this? What age did everyone switch from updating their status to mindless crap like what they cooked for dinner to suddenly bragging about this perfect life they seem to have and the perfect family?

There was a stage where I knew everyone was jealous of me, of my adventures and experiences.

I knew people were looking at me with envy as they worked their boring nine to five jobs and drove through the same streets day in, day out.

We were worlds apart – but now, they have everything I want.

Maybe they regret not taking the time to explore the world and experience everything it has to offer.

Maybe deep down they wish they had done what I was able to do, but they always look so content when I see them.

They're all so proud of the lives they have created for themselves. I know people only show you what they want you to see, so perhaps they are struggling with the way their lives have played out. But now I'm in my thirties and I have nothing to show for it. I have no money, no address, no friends, children or real career.

I don't have a relationship or someone to fall back on.

I don't have my twin sister.

The loneliness is whittling me down to nothing.

I remember a conversation Robyn and I had once, the last time I'd come down to visit.

We'd been sitting out on her porch watching the sun go down. "Maybe the way you are and the way you choose to live your life, maybe you don't need someone in your life," Robyn had said to me.

The way she said it made it sound like a fact.

Part of me had thought she was right at the time, but I had an overwhelming urge to prove her wrong.

I found Michael and I thought I'd done it. I was going to have my happily-ever-after, too.

I was going to catch up to everyone else. It was so close that I could actually taste it!

Now, I clench my hands into fists. I dig my nails deep into my palms until I pierce the skin. I watch as I bleed.

Maybe there's a part of me I didn't realise was there that actually finds solace in my loneliness.

I take my pills.

It isn't good when I get in my head like this.

I spiral out of control.

I help River to the front door and while she finds a spot in the garden to pee, I put a cigarette between my lips.

I know I need to make an appointment with a psychologist.

I need to talk to someone, make sure I don't lose it again.

I make a mental note to look up the doctors in the area later that day.

Smoke stings the back of my throat as I inhale. My fingernails are turning yellow. I wish smoking didn't feel so God-damned good.

In the distance I can see a few fishing boats bobbing up and down on the lagoon.

Shoals of fish ripple the surface of the water.

The pills are starting to take effect.

I feel myself relaxing. Unwinding.

That is until I peer into the bin where that speaker I'd thrown out should be. I chuck my cigarette to the floor and stomp it out as I rummage through the bin, just to make sure.

There's empty wine bottles and rotting banana skins there, but no speaker. It should be right on the top. It's the last thing I put in there!

I rifle through the trash. It has to be here.

Nothing.

I guess someone could have seen it and nabbed it from the bin.

I don't know what those things cost but surely someone would be eager to grab it if it was just lying there.

I try and tell myself that is exactly what happened.

Someone just took it from the bin – but I can't quite convince myself.

River cries from down in the garden, struggling to get back to the cottage.

I hurry over and carefully pick her up.

She's a tiny collie-dog. The runt of the litter. She weighs hardly anything in my arms.

I get her back indoors and lock up behind me.

Everyone's been told to keep their doors locked at all times now and to always check before opening up for anyone.

I put on another episode of Criminal Minds, wishing time would just stop.

I don't want to face the world tomorrow as a new week arrives.

I don't want to make an appointment with the doctor but if I don't, I know that things will get bad.

It turns out there's only one doctor in the area and she specializes in children.

I feel awkward sitting on the beige lumpy sofa, surrounded by toys and colourful posters on the wall.

I'm twiddling my thumbs, crossing and uncrossing my legs.

I feel exposed.

Dr. Georgia Pienaar is tapping her pen onto her notepad, looking at me through her wire-rimmed reading glasses.

Her hair is dyed an awful orange which clashes with her purple cardigan.

"What can I do for you today?" she asks me.

Her voice is sugar sweet.

How do I explain it?

I know this is a confidential session but I feel the need to ask her anyway. To make sure I can trust her.

She assures me everything I say will be kept between us unless I am a threat to myself or to others.

I don't even get two words out after that before I break down.

She hands me a box of lavender scented tissues and sits silently, staring at me. I blow and wipe my nose until it's raw and sore.

I tell her about Robyn, her disappearance.

I tell her there are literally no answers and that it is infuriating.

I tell her I feel helpless.

I bring up what happened to River and that stupid speaker.

I talk through sobs about Michael and Beatrix, their daughter.

The wedding I'll never have.

My infertility.

I talk about how left behind I feel from all of my friends who are creating these perfect lives for themselves, about how jealous it makes me whenever I log onto Facebook.

How much of a 'trigger' social media is for me.

How I see these pictures of proud parents bundling up their newborn babies, the pudgy little legs, the impossibly tiny fingernails.

What I would give to watch that silly Peppa Pig show on television parents are always complaining about with a child of my own.

I tell her about how just the sight of one of those gorgeous rabbit teddy bears with long floppy ears is enough to pull my heartstrings apart.

It gushes out of me like a tidal wave and when there are no words left I am out of breath.

I haven't told her about Luke.

I haven't told her about the journal or the threatening letter that was pinned to the shed when I found River.

A part of me wonders if that would be crossing the line over into uncharted territory.

Would she still keep things between us confidential if she thinks I have information that could help the investigation?

I just don't know. I need to tread carefully.

Her pen is flying across the open page of her notebook.

I peer over the page but all I can see are indecipherable scribbles.

Eventually she stops and sighs, places down her pen.

"Have you been to see a psychologist before, Piper?"

I nod.

She writes down the name of one of my previous doctors.

I don't give her all of them. I don't want her to find out about the blackouts.

I'm still trying to figure them out for myself. I know what she'd do. Send me off for a bunch of tests I can't afford, maybe throw me into an asylum.

I won't let that happen.

I also give her a list of some of the meds I'm on.

I notice her eyebrow cock when I mention the anti-psychotics.

Michael had given me the same reaction when I first told him, too. It's never been an easy thing to admit.

I want to scream at her, tell her she can't judge me.

"Can you tell me why you were prescribed that?" she asks.

I blink up at her, stutter a little.

"I- I had a few... *manic* episodes?"

I know I'm downplaying it.

I tell her about how much my miscarriages changed me.
Destroyed me, really.

I tell her more about the breakup with Michael. How he'd just deleted every photo of us he had from his Instagram page.

It made it look like I'd never been there at all. Like I'd never even existed.

How does someone do that to a person, I ask her.

How does someone just block you out like that?

It's cold. Hurtful doesn't even begin to describe it.

I tell her about how completely alone I've been feeling.

I need her to focus on that part of my life. I don't want her to go digging into my background too much.

She wouldn't like what she'd find out about me or my sister. That is my secret.

"Have you noticed a change since taking these pills?"

"My moods are better, for the most part, until lately I guess."

"Yes, a lot has been going on. It's understandable that you're struggling," she glances over the notes she's made. I wish I could see what she's written about me. I hate knowing she's forming an opinion of me and I can't even know what it is.

The urge to rip the notebook from her hands is intense.

I *need* to see what she's written.

I *need* to be in control.

"I do remember seeing both you and your sister in my practice when you were children. Do you remember that?" she looks up at me with a kind smile.

I don't remember. There is so much from my childhood that I can't recall. Don't want to recall. Won't recall.

"You were such naughty little things," her laugh is soft.

Tears sting my eyes. I grab another tissue and dab at my face.

Her expression turns serious.

"Piper, both you and Robyn had severe paranoia as children.
You'd been in and out of different foster homes, most of them bad," she's staring at me intently.

There's a flash of a memory. A man's large, hairy, calloused ridden hand in my knickers. My sister crying.

I squeeze my eyes shut.

I don't want to remember.

I can feel the panic rising like bile in my throat.

"Breathe." Her voice is firm, reassuring.

She knows she's cracking me open. *Bitch.*

I want a smoke.

I want to get away.

I don't even know how I'm going to afford this session.

I breathe in, hold it for a few seconds and then slowly exhale, just as she's telling me to do.

I do it again and again and again until I've slowed my heart-rate right down. Until it no longer feels like my heart is going to break straight through my breastbone.

When she can see I've calmed myself, she continues.

"How does it make you feel, remembering a bit of your past?"

"Scared," I say. I didn't even have to think about my answer. It wasn't a lie.

"Can you elaborate?"

I think for a moment.

"I haven't thought about it all in such a long time. I've been so proactive in keeping myself occupied."

She nods.

Rain is pouring outside, sliding down the windowpanes like tear drops.

"I guess I pushed it away for so long. I don't want to unearth those feelings I buried so long ago."

"Maybe it's the only way forward, to work through them."

"I feel guilty. I should have been there more for Robyn but I was always off doing my own thing," I say, trying to change the subject.

She takes the bait.

"Living your life isn't something you should feel at fault for."

There's a flash of lightning, a rumble of thunder.

"I could have called more often though, asked her how she was doing. When I read through our chat history I'm honestly ashamed. It was always all about me. I was always telling her about my news. Sometimes I didn't even bother asking how her life was going."

"Perhaps she didn't have anything new to say. You must remember you were off in new countries. You were planning your wedding. Things in your life were exciting and you wanted to share that with her," she makes it sound so reasonable, but it isn't.

"Right now, I'd give anything to just hear her voice. I'd let her talk about anything. What book she's reading, how her classes are going. What she's having for dinner. I just want to hear her talk. It doesn't matter if it's not exciting!"

There's so much regret in my voice.

"And then I feel even worse being sad about Michael as well. I shouldn't be thinking about him when there's something so much bigger than that going on."

"What do you think is going to make this better for you?"

"Her coming home?!" I scoff.

We chat about some exercises I should do.

She gives me some leaflets and a few website addresses to check out.

I feel like I've been scammed. She's supposed to be doing the work here, helping me. Instead, she's just pushing me over to a website filled with articles written by another doctor.

It infuriates me that she isn't doing her job properly. That she gets paid for this shit.

I know I won't look at the websites she's given me but I thank her anyway.

I think she can tell that there isn't an ounce of sincerity in my voice.

Forty-five minutes with her goes by at a snails pace.

I cannot wait to get out of there.

"Your anxiety is at an all time high. I am going to up your dose of quetiapine to eight-hundred milligrams a day. It will make you drowsy. No driving after taking it, OK?"

She rips a script out of a booklet and hands it to me.

"This is a short term thing. I want you to schedule in to see me again. We'll monitor it periodically, make sure you're doing okay." I nod.

In my hand, the script feels golden. This is what I needed.

I grab my umbrella and head to the reception area to settle the bill.

My phone pings when the transaction goes through. I almost thought it wouldn't.

Waiting for the card machine to print out the Approved slip had me biting my lip anxiously.

I can't bring myself to check the remaining balance in my account.

I have no idea how I'm going to get through the rest of the month, not after River's vet bills.

I've been living off of Cup a Soups and Pot Noodles and can feel myself becoming more malnourished by the day.

What I wouldn't do for some fresh vegetables.

Broccoli, asparagus, courgette's.

My mouth waters at the thought.

"What day next week suits you?" a young woman with a freshly snipped asymmetrical bob and a lip ring asks me.

"Tuesday, same time I guess," I shrug, watching her manicured fingers tap away on the keyboard.

My script is rolled up in my hand, ready for the pharmacist.

I finish making another appointment to see the doctor, but I doubt I'll actually turn up for it.

CHAPTER 9

At the pharmacy I peruse the shelves stacked with health foods and supplements. I grab a bottle of folic acid tablets and a new antiperspirant.

National Women's Day is around the corner and there are stands selling all sorts of fluffy slippers, scarves and mugs in various shades of pink.

Great little gifts for winter.

There's a selection of scented candles, Chilli Spice, Roasted Marshmallow and Island Rain. Little goodies to spoil women on a day created to eliminate discrimination against women.

I pick up a flyer about a march that's going to happen and pretend to read it.

I'm stalling, not wanting to get my prescription while there are other people nearby.

I don't want them to see what I have to take.

I wish the pharmacist could packet the medication behind the counter before giving it to me instead of putting it in an open plastic bowl for everyone to see.

"Ms. Brady!" Bibiana smiles at me. She's holding one of the candles in her hand.

My face is instantly aflame, remembering what she saw over the weekend. How she must think of me.

"How are you feeling?" she asks.

Her concern sounds fake.

Water droplets fall from her anorak onto the floor.

Everything is so silent I can hear the drips.

"Fine thanks," I rasp.

We're both in the dispensary queue, waiting to be dealt with.

I'm ahead of her. We stand in an unbearable silence while we wait.

Finally the pharmacist waves me over.

"You go ahead," I take a step back, practically pushing Bibiana in front of me.

"Oh, you sure?"

"Yes. You'll be late for class!" I say, desperate for an excuse.

She nods gratefully and hands the pharmacist her script.

He gives her a box. Of course I look.

Birth control. Of course.

I wonder if she's slept with Luke already.

I wonder what she'd think if she knew he's been with me.

Would she ever believe it? That someone like him could be with someone like me?

"See you in class!" she beams, unabashed by the box in her hand.

It's normal. I'm not.

I'm not normal at all.

I toss a tablet into my mouth and gulp it down with a bottle of sparkling water as soon as I get to my car.

I don't have to be at school for the whole day anyway and if I don't take this medication now, I know I won't cope.

*

I'm surprised to see Chloe back in class today.

There's fissures in her appearance. She looks exhausted, unkempt.

It's the first we've all seen her since the attack.

Her cheekbones have caved in. I can tell she's lost weight.

That usual glint in her eyes is gone.

She was already bony before, underweight even for a ballerina.

Now she looks terrible.

She keeps to herself, hidden behind an oversized hoodie that covers her face.

No one quite knows what to say to her.

She's not ready to dance again yet and has given her role to Bibiana.

As good as Bibiana is at dancing, she's no Chloe and she knows it.

"I'm so excited!" she trills to her group of friends, plucking at her new costume. She can't believe her luck. She's going to be the main girl.

They're like a pride of lionesses around her, excluding Chloe from the pack.

It's undeniable. Luke and Bibiana dance beautifully together.

It's incredibly intimate.

They have so much chemistry on stage it's hard to look away.

It's a hard sight to see for both me and Chloe... for very different reasons.

We're going through the routine, priming Bibiana for the role.

Luke's lifting her up high above his head, her petite little frame balancing effortlessly in his hands. He makes her look feather light.

They are both so focused, gliding along in perfect rhythm to the music.

The melody, the gentle tapping of her pointe shoes on the floor, the medication – it all mixes together and I feel, for just a moment, outside of my own body.

My eyes are heavy as I watch their bodies blur across the stage.

I lose track of time.

It could have been ten minutes or two hours – but suddenly I come back in to myself and the class is over.

I see Luke approach Chloe as the other students shuffle out of the room in pairs.

Their conversation is whispered, rushed. She's shaking her head, barely visible beneath the hood.

I can just hear her voice, low but vehement.

He's reaching out to touch her arm but she jerks away from him.

Bibiana is massaging her toes close-by, clearly trying to listen in.

I hear Chloe's voice rise an octave, she marches away from him and slams the door behind her.

I'm packing up the portable CD player (yes, I still have one of those), watching as Bibiana glides up to Luke.

"What was that all about?" she takes his hands in hers.

"Nothing important," he says.

I don't think they realise I'm still in the room, I've gone so quiet.

"Looked important," she sniffs sulkily.

He drops her hands. They fall to her sides.

She looks taken-back.

"Jealousy doesn't look good on you, babe," he says, walking out of the hall and leaving her behind.

Bibiana's jaw drops open, she's blinking rapidly.

"Prick..." I hear her say under her breath.

She's staring at the door, not quite sure what to do with herself.

"You OK?" I ask, sidling up to her with the CD player hoisted under my arm.

"Why wouldn't I be?" she shoots back, eyeing me testily.

I shrug.

"I've been in your position before," I tell her.

If only she knew how similar those positions were.

From the look on her face I can tell she doesn't believe me, or simply doesn't care.

She slings her backpack over her shoulder and as she's walking away from me I call after her.

"Well done today. You did great."

I mean it.

Luke has pulled completely away from me. He didn't look at me once throughout the day, in fact he flat out ignored me.

I'm confused as to why I feel hurt, rejected.

I'm angry at myself.

I should be thinking about the journal and nothing more.

It's not that I'm not thinking about the journal, but Luke was the first guy I slept with after Michael.

I hadn't realised until now the emotional implications that could have.

I don't want to feel this way but there's a sense of attachment there that I can't stand.

I try and tell myself he's a bad guy. He's done something to my sister. He's a player. Yet there's still that underlying part of me that wants to feel wanted by him.

I hate myself for it.

I have to fight against sending him a message and pestering him.

If he thinks I don't care then perhaps he'll come to me.

He seems like the kind of guy that likes the chase.

That's my new tactic.

The rain is still bucketing it down outside.

I'm grateful that I brought my car in today and don't have to make the walk home.

I turn the heater on in my car and watch all of the students filter out of the school doors and head to their cars.

I wait until mine is the last car in the parking lot, not wanting to leave anyone alone.

When I'm sure everyone has vacated I turn my key in the ignition.

I'm backing out of the lot when I see them together.

Luke's pinning Chloe against a tree.

It looks like she's struggling.

It's hard to see properly with the rain pelting down onto my windshield but I know something isn't right.

I cannot believe he is doing this in broad daylight. In public!

I rev my engine and speed over to the field, smacking my hand down onto the centre of the wheel. The hoot is deafeningly loud.

They pull apart violently. Chloe is gasping for breath.

I slam my car door behind me and run up to them.

"Are you OK?" I ask her, my eyes wild with worry.

She doesn't say anything, just stares between me and Luke.

Luke sighs in annoyance.

"We were just talking," he says, shaking his head at me.

His eyes are telling me things he cannot say. *Go away. Leave me alone, you psycho.*

"Didn't look like it," I'm firm. Ready with the pepper-spray clutched in my hand.

"I'm sorry Ms. Brady. We shouldn't have been doing that on campus." It's the first time Chloe speaks. Her cheeks are flushed.

Realisation dawns.

They were kissing.

I fumble for words, trying to compose myself.

Luke looks agitated, rubbing a hand across his mouth. Wiping away traces of Chloe's lipgloss,

"I – yes. No. You should not be doing that at school," I say.

My heartbeat is erratic.

"Sorry," Luke mutters, not meeting my eyes.

I have to seem like a teacher. I cannot make this seem personal.

"I'm going to have to give you both detention," I tell them and hear a collective groan.

The black spots that blur my vision are coming back.

The pills are weighing me down, taking over.

Humiliated, I get back into my car and pull away from them.

I shouldn't have done that.

The next day, Chloe is gone.

CHAPTER 10

The chloroform hadn't worked.
Chloe had thrashed around, fighting for her life.
I was surprised by the strength she had, given her tiny little body.
It was only when I'd been able to grab hold of the back of her
head, a fistful of her unwashed hair greasing up my hand, that I'd
been able to smash her face first into the brick wall.
Her pretty, pretty face.
Blood gushing everywhere, her head lolling on her shoulders
helplessly as I drive her to the location.
I drag her twitching body down to the rest of the girls, hearing
the thump, thump, thump of her limbs as I pull her down the
stairs. There's a crack of a bone, a shriek as she stirs with the
pain.
I rip the lanyard from around my neck and unlock the door.
"Welcome to the party," I grin, spittle spraying around the room
as I heave her up into a chair.
She's cradling her wrist. Yelps when I grab it and bind her hands
tightly behind the chair in a constrictor knot.
No way she'll be getting out of that.
She looks around the room, at the corps de ballet.
It is almost complete.
There's only a few more girls needed to complete the group.
One of the other girls in the room sobs, wisps of her hair falling
in front of her face. She's trying to scream through the duct tape

but I've wrapped it round and round her head too tightly for her to break through.

She doesn't stand a chance.

There's a scattering of rats. They're scrambling across the room, hiding behind the rusted drums and discarded cinder-blocks.

The putrid smell of mildew feels like home.

"Got a special treat for everyone tonight," I tell the girls, my breathing laboured from carrying the dead weight of Chloe down here.

Most of them barely acknowledge the arrival of a new girl. They're getting used to it now, accepting their fate.

I slide a big tub out of my backpack and open the lid.

The smell is rich and pungent. A melange of hearty flavours overpowers the stench of faeces for just a moment.

"Puttanesca. Whore's pasta!" I roar with laugh, watching all of the girls hungry eyes desperate for their supper.

I dig my hand into the tub, feeling the sauce and spaghetti squelch between my fingers. The sauce wedges under my fingernails like blood.

"So fitting, don't you think? Whore's pasta!" I nod at all of the snivelling whores in the room. I want them to get it.

Chloe is the only one without duct tape covering her mouth so I saunter up to her playfully.

"You've lost weight," I tut and ram a handful of the food into her face. She rejects it, turning her bloodied head away from me, mouth taut in disgust.

"How wasteful! You'll soon learn," I sneer at her.

The juice from the plum tomatoes dribbles down her chin.

"Won't she girls? She'll learn not to say no when it's feeding time!"

Some of the girls squeeze their tear-filled eyes shut as they nod.

I do love it when they cooperate.

I move on to the next girl. They don't have names anymore. Don't deserve them. Won't need them anyway.

I rip off the tape which tears a chunk of the girls hair off with it. She's so weak she can hardly cry out in pain as the roots are ripped from her scalp.

"Open wide," I say. She looks up at me fearfully, mouth wide open.

"There we go. Good girl," I say, jamming a handful of pasta into her mouth.

She moans, chews fast.

Opens her mouth for more.

"Don't be a greedy little slut," I say menacingly, watching her face contort into misery.

"Why are you doing this?" she croaks.

"Shut the fuck up!" I scream, pointing my finger at her gaunt face, full of olive oil.

I shove an anchovy from her cheek into her mouth and tape her up again. She chokes, struggling to swallow her food.

"See," I say, addressing Chloe. "This is how it's done."

I feed each of the girls just one mouthful.

Their stomachs growl for more, gurgling urgently throughout the room.

I hum one of the songs from Giselle's soundtrack, sitting in the centre of the room.

They all watch me produce a fork from my bag, a luxury they don't get anymore.

I twirl the spaghetti onto my fork and take a small, neat bite and chew thoughtfully.

I dab the corner of my mouth with a serviette.

I eat until I'm full.

There's still enough pasta in the tub to give everyone a full meal, but why would I do that?

I'm in a foul mood, after all.

I'd so been hoping to play with Piper a bit longer with the Alexa Echo system I'd set up, but the bitch threw it out on the very first night.

I'd even ordered a silly Halloween voice changing gadget online so that she wouldn't recognise my voice.

I'd been so looking forward to watching the poor thing go mad.

Good thing I'd picked it up out of the bin. I don't think I'm quite

done with it yet, or the journal. I nabbed that back, too.
There's still so much more fun to be had... in time.
Instead of actually feeding the whores their dinner, I place the tub on the floor right in the middle of them, just out of reach.
I leave them to stare at the food they can't get to. Let them watch in torture as flies land on top of the whore's pasta, rotting slowly away just like them.

Now they truly are the ghostly maidens from their roles in Giselle.

*

When I visit the girls again the following day, the top layer of the pasta has frozen over from the cold.
The girls teeth are chattering beneath the tape, the tips of their fingers are turning blue.
I decide to play a game.
I free their mouths and position the tub further away from them, right to the other end of the room.
"Let's see who can get to it first!" I'm cackling, spectating as they start to wriggle in their chairs.
Their primal instinct is to get to the food.
They are starving.
The first girl topples to the concrete, bashing her shoulder hard. There's a shrill cry but she's so hungry she continues to drag herself to the food, still bound to the chair. Slithering along the floor like a snake.
The other girls follow suit, all except for Chloe.
She's watching in a horrified silence as the girls she once knew start trying to attack each other in their chairs.
It is carnage!
They are ravenous and will do anything to be the first one to make it to the tub.
They are no longer friends.
Gone are the days of sharing a pizza over a bottle of wine, laughing and gossiping through the night.

They can't remember what it's like to share, they are fending only for themselves now. Couldn't care less if their best friend starves to death by their side.

Two make it to the tub at the same time and bash their heads together in mortal combat, both trying to dive into the frozen pasta.

They are grunting and growling at each other like animals.

Dogs fighting over a bone. Only one can win.

The other girls make their way there, biting at the first two girls bound ankles. Drawing blood.

One girl gets a chair leg to the eye. It pops right out of her socket and dangles curiously down her face.

There's a crunch as her nose is shattered, too.

I sit and watch, clapping in delight.

I pour a glass of wine to enjoy with the show.

The Corps de Ballet will soon become the Corpse de Ballet.

CHAPTER 11

A number of witnesses come forward to say they had last seen Chloe with Luke.

I have no other option other than to go in and tell them what I saw in the parking lot.

I cannot eat or sleep from the guilt. I should have stayed or offered her a lift home at least.

If I had, perhaps this wouldn't have happened.

The police take Luke in for questioning and he fast becomes the prime suspect.

His name is splashed all over social media as a person of interest.

Chloe's parents were caught on camera screaming at Luke as he was being led into the police station.

"Where is she?" Chloe's mother's voice was guttural.

Although he doesn't have an alibi for the evening of Chloe's disappearance, he seems to have proof of his whereabouts every night that one of the other girls went missing.

He was with Bibiana the evening Jessica went missing from her supposed date.

The sports teacher had confirmed Luke had been with him when Corrie had disappeared on her way to buy milk.

He had an answer for every evening besides Chloe's and with no hard evidence, the police had no other choice than to let him go.

He unwillingly made a statement to the press the next day.

He looked dishevelled as he looked into the camera and told the town that he promised he has nothing to do with this.

"Yes I was with Chloe the evening she went missing. We had

gone on a few dates before her first attack and I wanted to make sure she was OK when I saw her back at school for the first time," his eyes were ablaze with sincerity.

I stole a glance over at Bibiana while he made his speech.

She looked furious.

I wonder if she'd known Luke and Chloe had something before her. Or maybe even during...

He'd tried to go up to her after the statement was done but she'd pushed him away from her.

His head had dropped into his hands.

I had no idea what to think.

It's the first time I've seen genuine emotion on his face.

I hadn't told the police about what I'd found in his house.

The sex tape, the journal.

I could get fired or worse, arrested.

Luke being subordinate, I could be accused of so many things.

I could lose my teaching license.

It doesn't matter that I truly never tried to use my authority over him. Selfishly, I can't afford that to happen at the moment.

I still want to get my hands on the journal and find things out for myself before I go forward with what I have, but I still don't know how I could ever go forward regardless.

I see no way around the consequences and that makes me feel like an awful person.

That night I'm home with River, pouring over various newspaper articles on the missing girls. I'm sipping butternut soup from one of my mugs when there's a knock at the door.

River's head shoots up and she grumbles from her bed. She's not as boisterous as she once was.

I grab a cricket bat that I keep close to me at all times now and call out from behind the door.

"Whose there?"

There's a shuffle of feet, a clearing of a throat.

"It's me," Luke calls back. I grip the bat tighter.

"What do you want?" I ask, pulling my phone out of my back

pocket, ready to call the police.

River hobbles up by my side and sniffs at the door.

"Please... I have no where else to go." It sounds like he's crying.

I don't know why I do it. I feel like it's a scene from a horror movie. When the main character does something really stupid and you're sitting shouting at the screen, telling them not to open the door like they can actually hear you.

I unlock the door.

His face is ashen, his eyes swollen.

He looks at the cricket bat in my hands and his face crumples in despair.

"What happened to your dog?" he asks, looking down at River.

He's hovering in the doorway. I don't answer him.

Instead, I usher him inside and lock the door behind us.

I'm instantly aware of how messy the cottage is compared to his house. My shoes I'd kicked off earlier are lying on their sides. My dirty socks are strewn on the floor next to them.

There's a pile up of dishes I haven't bothered washing, some coffee cups growing peculiar looking things inside of them.

He follows me into the kitchen where I pour us each a glass of wine.

He notices the newspapers scattered across my sisters dining room table. There's one already printed with his face on it, an article about him being exonerated.

"My name is everywhere," he whispers.

I swipe the papers away and sit across from him.

"Are you OK?" I ask, not knowing what else to say.

He shakes his head.

"My life is ruined." Big fat tears fall down his cheeks.

I feel a surge of unexpected emotion for him.

I've never seen him look vulnerable before.

It's the first time he looks his age. It's the first time it hits me. This is just a boy. A seventeen year old boy.

It's as though I'd been hallucinating before. The man I had thought he was is no more.

"No one believes me, Piper."

Carefully, I reach my hand out and stroke his arm. I am not scared of him anymore.

River is lying by his feet. She can pick up his sadness.

"I'm not a bad guy!"

I tell him I know he isn't, even though I don't know that at all. Nothing adds up. The things I've seen and the things I've heard him say all scream otherwise.

"Have you read the article?" he gestures to the paper clipping with his photograph on it.

I nod my head slowly, watching as he grabs it from the pile of papers.

"Chloe Evans, seventeen, has gone missing from her local high school after last being spotted with fellow student, Luke Archer," he reads aloud, emphasizing his own name.

"The Evans family are desperately looking for answers after Luke was released from questioning at the station. Her alleged abduction is said to be connected to the recent disappearance of her dance teacher, Robyn Brady, shortly followed by the disappearances of her fellow classmates," he reads all of the missing girls names out to me even though he doesn't need to. I've memorized them all already.

"This is the sixth young lady to go missing from the area in just a few short months and the perpetrator is now being dubbed *The Pirouette Predator.*"

He stops reading, tosses the paper onto the table and takes a big gulp of the wine I gave him.

"My name is everywhere. I'm associated with this. My friends are looking at me differently. My mother phoned me in tears for fucks sake! She asked me if I did it! My own mother!" his hand slams onto the table, making me jump.

"I'm sorry," he places his hands to his lap and once again he looks like the lost boy I just let into my sisters home.

"Someone sprayed 'The Pirouette Predator' over my car in graffiti. I don't know what to do!" he's shaking his head, eyes darting all around the room.

I know what it feels like to be that paranoid. I wish I could tell him.

"Luke, what happened after I left the parking lot?"

"She blamed me for getting her in detention. Made a snarky comment and walked off. I told her she shouldn't be alone but she didn't want to be around me, either. Told me she'd spray me with the pepper-spray if I kept following her. I'd had enough so I let her be. She doesn't live far away from the school anyway, I thought she'd be fine!"

More tears splash onto the tabletop. I can see the guilt.

I think of the guilt I felt at leaving Chloe alone with Luke.

I don't know what to believe.

"You were kissing her before I got there," I say.

I'm not sure if it's a question or a statement.

"I was trying to, yeah. She didn't want me. She was pushing me away. That's when you turned up."

"What would have happened if I hadn't turned up?" I swirl the wine around in my glass, scared to look at him.

"I'm not a fucking rapist!" he yells.

River grumbles uncomfortably from under the table.

"I'm sorry!" my voice is placatory, my hands raised up.

"I like girls. I like sex. I hate being tied down but I swear I would never intentionally hurt someone, especially a woman. You have to believe me, Pip!"

"Then why the hell was my sisters journal in the drawer by your night-stand?!"

The words tumble out of my mouth before I can catch them. I gasp in shock.

Luke's eyes harden, his jaw clenches.

I can hear his teeth grinding back and forth as he mulls things over in his head.

"You went through my stuff. I knew it."

My hand reaches for the cricket bat but I knock it to the floor. It clatters noisily at our feet.

He stands, towering over me. River's grumbles become snarls but she doesn't move.

"I'm going to say this one more time," his eyes are bulging wide. I can see blood vessels in the whites of his eyes.

"I am not involved in this shit. I'm not going to fucking hurt you either!" he picks up the cricket bat and for a moment I think he's going to swing it right at my head.

I wait for the blow, wait for the crack and the splintering of wood. It doesn't come. He doesn't hit me.

Instead he places the bat into my trembling hands and lets me get a firm grip on the handle.

"Give me your phone," he demands, hand out.

I'm too frightened to not cooperate so I give it to him.

My lifeline.

He asks me to unlock it with my fingerprint. I offer him my thumb and watch as the phone screen lights up.

He punches in the emergency services number and hands the phone back to me.

He sits back down.

"Feel safer now?" he sounds sarcastic, like he can't quite believe I feel this way about him.

"I'm going to tell you something and I need you to listen closely," he says.

I nod. There's nothing else I can do. I have the bat. I have the phone. I try to let these things comfort me but I'm still petrified. I don't know if this is a trick. River has reverted back to her unsure grumbles under the table.

"Someone has been planting weird shit in my house. Girls underwear, your sisters journal. I don't know where they are coming from. Someone keeps sending me anonymous messages. I get these fucked up notes pinned under my windscreen wipers and nailed to my front door," he produces his phone and hands it to me.

There's a handful of messages dated before Chloe's disappearance.

Don't worry, I'm getting rid of the Corps de Ballet. All for you.
The first message read. I frown as I scroll on.

You'll see the news tomorrow. Another one bites the dust. This one was a fighter! Can see why you liked her.

They go on like this. Cryptic little text messages giving nothing much away.
It's the last message that makes me feel off-balance.

Leave Piper alone or she's next.

Seeing my name on Luke's phone makes my pupils dilate. I wipe a sheen of sweat from my forehead, my pulse rapid. The message is a threat telling him to leave me alone.
Someone knows about us.
That's why he's been so distant.
Everything is suddenly starting to make sense. The way he has been treating me – I wasn't imagining it. He was ignoring me because he was trying to protect me.
"What the hell is this?" I'm breathless.
I try to scroll on but there's nothing more.
"I don't know. There's handwritten notes too. I don't have them on me but I've kept them all," Luke says, taking his phone back.
I grab the wine and drain the glass.
"Why haven't you gone to the police?" I ask.
"I thought it was a stupid prank at first. A mate, Steve probably, being an idiot," he shrugs at me.
"When I started getting the messages about some of the girls disappearing before anyone else knew about it, that's when I realised this was serious. But the notes nailed to my door are covered in blood. It kind of looks like they've been written in blood, really. They said stuff like, 'Go to the police and I'll gut you in your sleep.'" he looks ashamed.
"You were too scared to come forward," I say.
I tell him I understand. I tell him about the note I had on the door of the shed where I found River.
He's the first person I've told the whole truth to.
It instantly lifts a weight from my shoulders to share it with

someone. To speak the words out loud. Even to Luke.

He shivers.

"If someone can do that to a dog, I don't know what the fuck they could do to someone like me." He's shaking his head like he can't quite believe it.

"Or to all the missing girls," I remind him.

He pushes his thumb and forefinger into his eyes. It looks like he's in agony.

"Can I have my sisters journal back?"

"It's gone. I think. It's not where I found it. I'm so fucking paranoid someone's going to come into my house and find all this shit that I have nothing to do with. I feel like I'm being set up!" He's pulling at his hair, his voice wobbling.

I have no idea if he's telling the truth or not. If he isn't, he's a damn good actor.

"There's something else," he says reluctantly.

I swivel around to face him, the wine bottle in my hand. I was just about to top us both up.

"What is it?" I ask.

I can tell straight away that he doesn't want to tell me.

I don't move.

"The thing is..." he pauses, looks away from me. His rubs his hand vigorously through his hair and sighs.

"All the girls that have been taken so far, your sister included... I've been with them all."

"As in, you've slept with them all?"

He winces, nods.

"At first I thought it was just coincidence! The real connection seemed to be that they were all dancers... but what if it's more to do with me? I know that sounds arrogant. I'm sorry, I'm over-thinking it," he shakes his head, embarrassed.

I chew on the inside of my cheek.

"The police already suspect me. I can't have them finding out that I've been with literally every girl taken so far, but at the same time I think I need to go to them before this shit goes any further."

Panic explodes inside of me as he says this.

"Luke, no! You cannot go to the police," I grab his hands in mine.

"Why?" his voice is a whisper.

I think for a moment, trying to figure out the best way to keep his mouth shut.

"If you go to them, you'll have to tell them about us. They'll find the message about me on your phone and ask you about it. Luke, that could get me in serious trouble, don't you see that? I could end up in prison!"

"I'll delete the message mentioning you."

"If the police seize your phone they can recover deleted messages Luke," I say. *Idiot*.

"But people could be dying!" he shouts back at me, tugging at his hair.

"I know. I know that. I'm sorry. Just, lets think about this for a bit. OK?" I stare right into his eyes, still not sure how the hell I'm going to convince him not to go to the police.

Thankfully, he nods and we sit in silence for a while.

I don't want to ask the next question, but I do anyway.

"Luke, who else have you been with that dances at school?"

He's shaking as he looks up at me.

He pushes the wine glass around on the table before picking it up and bringing it to his lips.

"All of them," he whispers, quickly gulping down the Shiraz.

CHAPTER 12

I love you so much, it hurts.
I wonder who the first person to ever say those words was.
There was a singer in the forties who wrote a song about it, Floyd Tillman.
I listen to that song on repeat these days with all the whores around me. I lie in the centre of them forlornly, like a love sick puppy, thinking of you.
Tillman's voice is haunting as it echoes throughout the basement. It's really quite a charming song.
From the words, I feel like Tillman just understands me. Understands us. Understands what I'm going through in order to be with you again.

I'm waiting for the day we can finally be together again, my love. It hurts me so that I have to wait this way.
It is bitter sweet though, because I know our forever is coming soon.

I just have to be patient.

My phone rings. Again.
It's been ringing incessantly all day.
I want to tell everybody to leave me alone.

I'm busy!
I role my eyes and ignore the call.
The girls all around me stare at the phone like it's the holy grail...
and I guess to them, it is.

Such a pity I won't let them near it, isn't it?

CHAPTER 13

I wake tangled up in my bedsheets, Luke's arm slung over me.
He's snoring softly.
I take the moment to look at him properly.
His eyelids flicker as he dreams, his mouth slightly open.
I count the freckles sprinkled across the bridge of his nose.
His nostrils slowly flare as he exhales and his lips twitch.
Last night plays over and over again in my head.
How genuine he seemed. The fear I saw in his eyes.
Now he looks so peaceful, like he's finally let go and can rest.
I like that he feels safe with me.
I like that he tried to make me feel safe with him.
I still have no clue what I'm doing. I'm working myself up for
heartbreak if I continue this.
We could never work.
I know I'm over-thinking it but I just can't stop. Cody is better
suited for me. We're the same age. It isn't illegal.
I sigh, shaking my head as these thoughts fly through my mind.
He stirs when I try to slide out from under his arm.
"Morning," he blinks up at me, rubbing the sleep from his eyes.
He pulls me in for a kiss. His morning breath doesn't bother me.
His hands grasp at the back of my head, his fingers intertwining
with my hair.
"Thanks for last night," he whispers into my ear.
I hadn't intended on sleeping with him. Not after what he'd told
me – but he'd broken down right at the table in front of me.

Tears had streamed down his blotchy face.

He'd tried to hide it from me but the bottle of wine we'd finished together had loosened him up.

It had loosened me up, too.

I'd gone around the table to hug him. I put my arms around his shoulders and pulled him in to me.

He fell into my arms like a small boy. It was the first time in a while I felt needed.

I could feel his relief at being held.

He could sense my relief in being needed.

We were two broken parts coming together, helping each other when we both needed it the most.

"It's OK," I'd soothed, kissing his forehead lightly.

He looked so scared. I cradled him for what seemed like hours, until he'd fallen asleep in my bed.

His eyes are still puffy now from crying and exhaustion.

"I'll make us some coffee," I smile shyly as I slip out of the bedroom, self-conscious about the pyjama shorts I'd wriggled into last night.

Michael was the last person I'd woken up to and he was used to seeing me dressed down, hair up and with a clean face.

I worry Luke will look at me and wonder why the hell he's in my bed when he sees me without my usual work clothes and make-up – but he barely seems to notice.

It all seems surreal and oddly normal.

River wags her tail at me as I come into the kitchen and gives my hand an excited lick, like she hasn't seen me for ages.

I flick on the kettle and scoop some pellets into her bowl before opening the back door for her.

I stir honey into the coffees, watching River hop around the garden. She's getting more mobile on three legs now, although I can see she still struggles.

There's so much going on right now yet despite it all I catch myself singing under my breath, like I'm in my own little unpoppable bubble.

While my head should be thinking about the threats, Robyn and the other missing girls and my financial crisis, I'm focusing on the positive. I wonder if the higher dosage of medicine is responsible for my momentary bliss.

For just one moment everything seems calm. As it should be.

"Knock knock!"

There's a rapping of knuckles against the door. I spin around and see Cody standing just outside.

I drop the teaspoon I was holding in shock.

"Hi!" I breathe.

"Sorry, I startled you!" he laughs softly.

I lean against the counter, hoping Luke won't come out into the kitchen.

The cottage is open plan. The kitchen connects into the living room with no door between them. There's only a short hallway leading down to the bedrooms. My mouth goes dry.

The reminiscence from last night is all over the place.

The empty wine bottle, two glasses by its side. Luke's shoes are just out of Cody's sight.

"Have some company last night?" Cody asks me.

His voice is friendly enough but I feel instantly invaded.

"Yeah. Old friend popped over," I giggle nervously.

His eyebrow hitches as he nods. He knows I have no friends here. He looks me up and down.

My shorts cling to my thighs and my baggy t-shirt has holes in the sleeves. I'm barefoot and my hair is twirled up into a messy bun. I suddenly feel the need to cover myself up.

"I just wanted to see if you wanted to get some coffee before work?" he says slowly.

I'm not sure who's more embarrassed at seeing me like this, him or me.

"Oh, no thanks! I just made a cup," I gesture towards the coffee. My heart stops.

He sees the two coffee cups next to the kettle, not just one.

"Sure. See you in class," he gives me a sombre look that riddles me with guilt.

I watch him pat River on the head as he walks away.

Two days later an envelope drops through my letterbox. It lands with a thud onto the dusty wooden floorboards.

River hobbles up to it, sniffing at it curiously.

"What is it River?" I ask her, rubbing behind her ears as I pick up the envelope.

My name is scrawled across it in pretty handwriting that looks curiously like mine. The envelope is thick and heavy in my hands. I tear it open from the glue, letting a stack of photographs fall out onto the floor.

I crouch down to pick them all up and freeze.

I'm stunned.

I can't breathe.

I'm teetering on the edge of sanity.

The first photograph I see is one of Luke outside of my sisters front door.

The next is of me opening the door. I'm wearing the ripped jeans, white strap top and coral blazer I'd been wearing the other day. The cricket bat is in my hand.

The third photograph is of me letting him in.

There's a growing pain in my chest as I flick through more of them.

Us at the table, drinking wine.

Me hugging him, my body pressed right up against his.

His head buried into my chest.

The next one is graphic. I'm on top of him, naked.

It's so close that I can see scratches on my back from his nails as he'd pulled me down to him. How had someone taken these?

The last one is of both of us asleep in my bed. It looks like it was taken from inside the cottage. How did someone get in here? How had River not noticed?

Bile rises in my throat. This is bad. There's a note scribbled on the back of the last photograph.

'There are more of these. Stop looking for me or I will make sure

everyone sees them.'

I run to the windows and close all of the curtains, my mind racing.

I lock every door. Dash through the cottage, checking every room to make sure I am alone like I used to do as a child if our foster mother went out and left us alone.

I feel trapped.

Someone is watching me.

Someone could give these to the headmaster or to the police.

My life would be ruined. I'd lose everything. Again.

I am so ashamed. What have I done?

I can hardly walk as I make my way to the bathroom.

I open the cabinet and take a handful of pills with a big gulp of water straight from the tap.

I wait for my heart rate to ease, slumped on the floor.

I think about Robyn. How I used to rock her back and forth in my arms when the paranoia would take hold of her in the big, empty house.

I wish I had someone to do that for me right now.

I light a fire and burn the photographs one by one. I watch the flames lick the edges of the shots and curl around them like a blanket.

I cannot take any chances.

Even though I know there will be copies out there somewhere, I have to get rid of any form of evidence in my sisters cottage.

CHAPTER 14

Drugging that dog was incredibly easy. Piper really needs to teach it not to accept food from strangers.
It amazes me how vulnerable everyone is.
The photographs were even easier.
Piper doesn't even realise how many camera I've hidden in and around the place.
There's video footage too.
It repulses me to watch her that way... opening her legs up like another stupid whore. I don't care that she doesn't dance, after what she's done she deserves to join the others.
She is such a disappointment.

You'd think they'd have given me a better name.
'The Pirouette Predator,' what a joke! I was expecting, 'The Ballerina Butcher'. Something with a bit more of a ring to it.
I think of the serial killer nicknames I know, Helter Skelter, The Zodiac Killer or something like 'Doctor Death' from that podcast I'd loved listening to a while ago.
I wonder if other serial killers were happy with the names they got.
Mine sounds so juvenile.
I guess in my case there haven't been any bodies yet.
Oh, but there will be and it is going to be glorious.
Adrenalin pulses through me at the thought of my first kill.

I wonder who I should choose first.
Eenie meenie miney mo.
Chloe is by far the most annoying.
She hasn't eaten anything I've tried to give her.
Every time I try to give her something she spits at me. I could
choose her – but watching her slowly break seems like so much
more fun.

I spear the last few chickpeas onto my fork before dumping my
plate on the ground beside me.
My hands are blackened from dirt and there's soil under my
fingernails.
I pick up the shovel and continue to dig.
Six perfect graves side by side.
I wish I could get the whores to help. How fun it would be to
watch them dig their own graves – but I cannot trust them if I
remove their bindings and I definitely can't trust them with a
shovel in their hands.
I keep changing my mind.
I can't quite decide how I want their bodies to be discovered.
If I bury them it will be longer until someone stumbles across
them.
Their bodies will have decomposed so much that all of my hard
work of fattening them up will be for nothing besides my own
satisfaction.
Perhaps I can photograph them, leave shots of how they last
looked on top of their rotting corpses.
I contemplate this as I continue to dig out in the cold, sleet
making it near impossible to see right in front of me.

To be honest, I am second guessing myself just a little bit.
Can I really kill them? I've never killed anyone before.
This is all so new and exciting for me.
It's a bit like a game. A challenge, shall we say.
Do I have what it takes? Can I do it?
I suppose the graves are a comfort blanket for me. If I do kill

them, I don't want to be left freaking out and without a plan.
As sinister as my mind may be, I'm not sure I can do the whole dismembering a body thing. I've heard about it before and it just sounds vile.
I don't like to get my hands too dirty.
This new life of mine is fascinating, really.
I am learning so much about myself.
I could just speed up the process and each day plunge a knife into one of their chests. I could make them watch each other slowly bleed out, anticipating the next day and the next death.
They'll never know when it will be their turn.
Eenie meenie miney mo.
I smile wickedly, exhilarated by my thoughts.
I toss the shovel to one side and skip down into the basement to see my whores.
It's time to choose the first girl.
It's time to put me to the test.
I untie one of them, she's so weak that her arms flop to her sides uselessly. She can hardly raise her filthy head to look at me.
I grab her chin and inspect her, holding a knife in my hand.
I draw the blade across her lips, just enough for it to tickle.
She tries to jerk away from me but I hold her still.
"Don't try to fight me, sweetheart," I tell her pityingly.
The other girls are fearfully watching, grateful it isn't them.
Selfish, all of them.
I brush the knife down her neck, over her collarbone and torso until I reach her bound feet.
Her toenails are so long they've curled into her skin.
I grab her left foot and hold it firmly in my hand.
Dancing has taken its toll on her feet. They're deformed with bunions – yet these feet can still do such beautiful things on pointe.
She's trembling as she looks down at me holding the blade against her toes.
"Shall we play 'This Little Piggy?'" I laugh, wiggling a toe between my thumb and forefinger.

I'm almost drooling with anticipation.
"This little piggy went to the market..." I sing.
"This little piggy stayed home! This little piggy had roast beef and this little piggy had none," I pull a sad face.
All of the girls are watching. Waiting.
"And this little piggy..." I'm snarling now, gripping the knife tighter and tighter as it edges closer to the whores baby toe.
"Went WEE, WEE, WEE!" I slice the toe effortlessly off.
It falls pathetically to the cold concrete floor.
The girl is writhing in pain, her screams so violent under the masking tape she almost breaks free. All of the other girls start squirming in their seats, both sobbing and trying to scream too.
"All the way home," I finish with a smile.
Blood gushes freely from her foot as she looks down at her severed toe.
There is so much adrenalin coursing through my veins I almost don't hear the footsteps coming from outside.
My head snaps up to the boarded up window. I can make out the shadow of a figure walking around close to the graves I've been digging.
The girls are in an uproar, trying as hard as they can to make noise.
"Shut up!" I hiss at them. There's blood all over my hands.
I can hear the crunching of gravel, the sound of voices.
Two people.
They are so close.
"If ANY of you make a sound, I WILL saw your toes off one by one," I wave the knife at them.
I wipe the blood onto my jeans and trudge irritatedly up the staircase.
An elderly couple is standing right over the open graves. The woman is pointing and saying something I can't hear to the man by her side.
He's reaching into his pocket.
My heart is beating excessively.
He pulls out a cellphone and starts punching in a number.

I growl under my breath, my hackles rising as I stomp towards the shovel I'd tossed outside the door on my way down to the girls.

They are so preoccupied with their discovery they don't even hear me coming up behind them.

"Hi there!' I call in a friendly voice from behind them.

They turn on their heels to face me.

The old woman's mouth drops open at the sight of my bloodstained clothing.

The shovel is above my head and in one quick swing I connect it with the man's head.

My entire arm vibrates from the impact as the man falls to the floor, the phone clattering down with him.

The woman lets out a piercing shriek.

CHAPTER 15

No one can quite believe it when two more people are reported missing.

They, unlike the others, aren't dancers. They were just an elderly couple out for an afternoon walk from the retirement village and they never came back.

This time it's their faces splashed across the newspapers and television.

I listen to a news-reporter talk about the couple and speculate as to whether their case is connected to the others.

I'm waiting in the pub for Cody, who has asked me to meet him here for a chat.

I couldn't keep avoiding him forever.

The smell of beer permeates the air.

I'm desperate for a drink after the day at school.

Naturally, none of the students could focus on anything other than the two new disappearances.

It's all anyone could talk about.

Luke hasn't been to class since being questioned by the police. Too embarrassed to show himself.

I drove past his car on my way to the pub. It was parked at a garage and a handful of men were scrubbing at the graffiti covering the one side. 'The Pirouette Predator' is still easily readable across the doors.

He'd called me the day I received the envelope with the photographs of us.

He got the same envelope in his post.

"This is completely fucked," his voice had crackled down the other end of the phone.

I didn't know what to say.

"I can't do this anymore," he'd sighed and hung up on me. We haven't spoken since. It was inevitable, really.

When Cody comes in he orders us each a drink and sits down across from me. He looks tired, with deep dark rings under his eyes.

"Why did you kiss me?" he asks, getting right to the point.

I stammer, not sure what to say.

'I was drunk,' hardly seems like a response he'd appreciate.

Instead, I decide to be as honest as I can be.

"I don't know, Cody. I've been so stressed out and you looked after me so nicely it just kind of happened," I say, not looking him in the eyes.

"Piper I like you. A lot. I worry about you living alone and being by yourself a lot."

"I have River," I remind him.

"That's not the point. I want to look after you."

No one has looked after me in such a long time.

The words are hard to hear and believe.

"Cody, it was just a kiss," I feel terrible saying it, but it's true.

"But-" he starts, but I interrupt him.

"There's more important things right now than this! Can't you see that? My sister is missing! All those students. The old couple. My dog. The threats!" I blurt out.

"Threats?" his eyes are boring into my own.

I rub my temple, trying to collect myself. I can't let things slip out like this.

"I meant River. Her leg," I lie.

"You told me she got hit by a car. What threat?" he looks confused.

There's too many things in my head, it's overwhelming.

I can't think straight.

My phone rings.

"Piper?" he presses.

"Just stop it!" I shout, jumping up out of the booth.

I look down at my phone, at who is calling me.

It's Dr. Georgia Pienaar. I missed our session.

I know she's trying to check in on me.

I can't afford her. I press ignore.

"I can't handle you constantly being around me, trying to get involved! Stop, please!" my voice is a high-pitched hiss that turns heads around the bar.

"Piper, what the hell?" he calls after me as I dash out of the pub, leaving my last drink untouched.

I have to be more careful.

*

The text messages from Cody stream in throughout the evening.

Can you please tell me what you were talking about. Is someone threatening you?

What really happened to River?

Piper, please just let me know you're OK.

I ignore them all.

I've locked myself inside the cottage, drawn all the curtains closed and am hugging my knees to my chest in bed.

I'm trawling through Facebook. So many of the students don't privatize their accounts so everything they post is available for the world to see.

I click onto Bibiana's profile. Her main photo is one of her dancing, naturally.

She posted a photograph of her and Luke just a few weeks ago and among the thumbs up there were a few angry and sad faces left there by other girls.

It really does fascinate me how open people are on social media.
I scroll to her latest status update.

*Folks out of town for the night, gone off on one of their safari
excursions again (eye-roll). Anyone up for a girls night?!*

I want to tell her to delete the post.

She could be publicly handing herself over to the '*Pirouette
Predator'* or whatever he's called with what she's put out there.
It's literally telling everyone that she's alone at home tonight.
There's a few comments on the post.

One of her friends, Verity, a dark-skinned girl I don't recognise
has told her she'll be right over with a bottle of wine.

One of the boys, Steve has left a snide remark asking them why
they aren't studying or doing something useful with their time.
Three angry faces appear alongside it.

My phone buzzes again.

I'm coming over.

He's too much. After being alone for a while now, it feels weird
having someone pandering after me this way.

Even when I was with Michael we were never a couple that
continuously checked in on each other throughout the day.

He hardly ever knew my movements, where I was or who I was
with and vice versa.

When Cody knocks on the door I ignore it. He knows I'm inside,
my cars parked in the driveway.

I make a cursory glance at the door, listening to him trying to
coax me outside.

"Piper, let me in," he's come around to the side of the cottage.
He's standing right outside the bedroom window. Luckily the
curtains are drawn.

River looks at me curiously. She recognises his voice now.

I think back to how close I felt to Cody the night we shared that
pricey bottle of wine around his oak barrel.

I shouldn't have let myself get so friendly with him.

"Let me help you. If someone's threatening you, lets go to the

police!"
I pull the blanket around myself and wait for him to leave.
When I'm sure he's gone I roll over onto my side and sigh.
The silence is a comfort.
I've just drifted off when a voice speaks up.
"Goodnight, Piper."
It's the same voice I'd heard before.
I freeze, my eyes struggling to adjust in the darkness.
My hand swipes at the bedside table but there's no speaker on it.
The voice sounded so close.
Someone is in the room.
I start to scream, hoping the neighbours will hear me.
I scream so loudly I think I'm going to shatter my vocal chords,
but I don't stop.
River starts to bark and snarl from down the hallway.
The room starts to slowly become more visible.
I look around me and see nothing, but I know I heard that voice.
I'm still screaming, my voice breaking as I charge to the front
door. I try to open it but it's locked.
I hammer my fist against it and hurtle into the kitchen to find the
keys. They're not where I left them.
I try the back door but that is locked too.
I'm trapped.
"Help!" I scream louder and louder, banging on the door.
River is panicking by my side, her barking sharp in my ears.
I'm petrified to look over my shoulder. I can *feel* eyes on me.
I know someone is watching me.
I hear the front door being kicked in. Splinters of wood go flying
in all directions.
I hear footsteps running through the house, following my
screams.
When I see the police officers I collapse onto the floor, my voice
finally resting.
I close my eyes.
I'm safe now.

Detective Engelbrecht sits me down and gives me a cup of sugared water while Jensen searches the house.

River is anxiously limping around us, unable to relax.

"Have you been drinking again this evening Ms. Brady?" he asks me bluntly.

"No," I lie.

I don't want them to get the wrong idea of me.

"OK. What were you doing this evening?" he probes.

I'm not a good liar. I pause for a second too long.

"I stayed in. I've just been watching TV," I say.

"So this receipt from a bar with today's date on it doesn't belong to you?" he holds up a slip of paper and waves it in my face.

Fuck.

I must have dumped the receipt on the counter when I got back home.

"Three *double* gin and tonics *and* a glass of wine," he reads.

I don't know what to say. I don't remember having that much to drink.

Cody bought me a drink at the bar and I'd barely touched it before storming out.

I don't feel like I've had that much to drink, but I must have.

"Look, yes! I went out. I had a drink with a work colleague, but I'm not drunk! You can see that," I gesture at myself wildly.

"I beg to differ," Jensen says.

Engelbrecht gives him a subtle cough and a stern look.

"Please," I beg.

"You have got to believe me. I heard that voice again. I swear I did."

Both of their arms are crossed as they look down at me.

"What would you like us to do here, Miss?"

"Read you a bedtime story? Check there's no monsters under the bed?" Jensen sniggers. I'm developing a deep distaste for him.

"That's it. Get out," Engelbrecht points at the door that's off its hinges.

There's someone on their way over to fix it temporarily for the night. I'll need to get a new door sorted tomorrow.

I wonder if that's another expenditure I'll need to fork out money I don't have for or if the police will foot the bill.

"Thank you," I whisper at him, grateful that Jensen's gone.

"You've put us in a really awkward spot, Ms. Brady," he says.

"Please believe me. I'm telling you the truth!"

He sighs.

"Mind if I take a look around?" he finally asks me.

I shrug, lacing with fingers together as he walks out of the kitchen.

I try to calm River down as he searches the cottage.

He's only gone for a few minutes. When he reappears, the speaker and my set of house keys are in his hands.

"Found these under your bed," his lip twitches.

His stare is boring into me.

I shake my head in bewilderment.

"I didn't put them there!"

I can tell he doesn't believe me.

He drops the keys onto the table in front of me. The key chain thumps down hard onto the wood, a hand carved lemur that I'd bought from a little market in Madagascar with Michael.

It was from our last trip together. I still haven't been able to remove it from my keys. Still in denial.

I stare at it now, unable to meet the officers eyes.

"If you don't mind, I'll take this," he's still holding the speaker in his hand.

I nod silently.

I want nothing to do with that thing.

"I threw it away. I put it in the bin outside and the next day it was gone. I'm telling you someone is getting into this place and planting shit. Someone is doing this to me!"

I'm hysterical now, but all he does is sigh. Again.

He's had enough.

He stays with me up until the repair guy has boarded up the door securely... as if that's going to help me sleep any better tonight.

I end up staring at the ceiling, jumping at every little sound until my eyes are dry and bloodshot.

CHAPTER 16

When day breaks, I am absolutely exhausted.

Running purely on caffeine, I make my way to school.

I can't stop thinking about that Alexa Echo speaker and my house keys under the bed.

How is someone getting in?

I know it's not really my place to do it, but I swing by the local locksmith on my walk.

The signage is old, as though it hasn't been changed for over twenty years. You can just make out the name of the company, Evans Locksmith. It is, like the rest of this town, antiquated.

The man behind the counter agrees to change all of the locks on the doors after I tell him a bit of my story.

"Used to know your sister, Robyn," he grumbles as he takes down some details on a worn leather notebook.

"Oh yeah?" my interest piqued.

I study the wrinkles embedded in his forehead as he drops his pen to the paper.

"She taught my daughter in school," he chews him lip, not meeting my eyes. He looks deep in thought.

"Ah, right. Well, I'm probably teaching her now then. I've taken over for a while," I give him a smile he doesn't return.

I watch his shoulders droop.

"She's gone," he whispers, his sniff startling me.

"Gone?"

"He took her," he slams his hand down onto the counter-top.

I back away slightly. He looks up at me, his cataract ridden eyes are haunted.

"He?" I ask, my voice wavering.

"Luke took Chloe. I know he did. I told her from the start that boy was trouble. I swear I'm going to kill that son of a bitch myself."

With that, he rips an invoice out of his pad and hands it to me.

"I'm so sorry. I had no idea-" I start, mortified that I didn't realise that he's Chloe's dad. Paul Evans.

Evans Locksmiths.

How hadn't I realised that?

I should have known. It's such a small village.

Everyone knows everyone here.

I eye him guiltily as I pocket the invoice.

"I'll be over this afternoon to change your locks, Ms. Brady."

Bibiana and Verity aren't at their desks in the classroom when I arrive.

We've had to implement a role call at every class now. If one of the students is missing from class we have to inform the headmaster. He then sends out people to search for them if they'd been in earlier classes or, if not, their parents are immediately called to make sure they are OK.

I'm too worried about how I'd explain myself, stalking my students online. The headmaster would want to know how I knew about the 'Girls Night' the girls had planned.

Luckily, I don't have to.

A couple of the other students mention it and the police are sent to Bibiana's place straight away.

It isn't long before the news breaks.

When they had arrived, they saw a large windowpane by the kitchen completely shattered.

There was a muddy footprint on the windowsill where someone had climbed through.

A brick lay in the middle of the floor. It had been thrown through the window and connected with the marble counter-top.

Whoever flung it must have done it at full force because the marble was dented.

Whoever had done it certainly wasn't worried about making a noise...

Both of the girls were gone.

Their handbags had been ransacked.

Police could only assume someone had taken any money inside their purses because all of their cards and cellphones were still there.

The house was cordoned off as forensics came in to investigate.

The footprint was analysed.

It belonged to someone with a minuscule sized foot and the sole of the shoe appeared to be a female brand, not male.

The police gave a statement saying that their hope was that one of the girls, Bibiana or Verity, had managed to climb through the window and get away from the abductor.

They were still waiting for confirmation on Verity's shoe size to see if it could be a plausible theory.

People online were in an uproar, desperate to have their say.

If one of them managed to escape, where is she now? Someone had asked.

Hundreds of comments followed suit.

Some said she must be hiding, others wondered if she was somehow involved.

Can someone tell me how the parents could leave their daughter alone for a night while they go gallivanting off to the bush to watch some stupid zebra grazing in a field? While there's a psychopath on the loose!?

That comment had over seventy likes.

I wonder if Bibiana's parents had seen it.

I wonder what they are thinking.

How can ONE person abduct two people?! There must be an accomplice, right? Another student had asked.

One of my other dancers, Britt, had replied to him asking him if he'd ever seen 'those true crime documentaries.'

She pointed out that it is more than possible for someone to kidnap two people at once.

Glad I didn't join the party! Another girl had added, with a relieved looking emoticon next to her comment.

A bunch of people told her they were going to 'unfriend' her because of her comment.

The bickering was constant.

Helicopters were sent up to search for the missing girls but returned with no sightings. No answers.

They had vanished into thin air, just like the rest of the girls.

In the house there were absolutely no fingerprints found.

The only thing they had to go on was that one clear footprint.

Cadaver dogs have been scouring the streets and nearby forest, but even they can't seem to pick anything up.

It looked like the girls had been watching the film, Black Swan, starring Natalie Portman.

It's a movie Robyn used to love when we still lived together.

She used to make me watch it at least once every few months.

We'd huddle up on the sofa, a plate of celery sticks and mixed berries between us as we sipped on a glass of wine each and watched the movie.

I feel a surge of shock rush through my body as I think about my sister. Sometimes I still can't quite believe that she's one of the missing girls. Sometimes it still hits me.

She's gone.

Bibiana and Verity's wine goblets were sticky with lipstick, the bottle half empty on the coffee table in front of the television.

I feel like I've failed. I should have said something.

I felt this one coming. I sensed it.

Why didn't I say anything?

Useless. Useless. Useless.

I slap my head with my hands, admonishing myself for being so stupid.

Even though I'm rattled by what happened to me last night, I have to carry on.

I'm busy prepping for my next class when Cody comes into the room.

I look at him through my spectacles that are slipping down the bridge of my nose.

"Cody-" I start, watching as he closes the door to the classroom behind him.

I stand up from my seat.

He walks towards me and before I know it his big hands are grabbing my jaw. I try to pull back but he pulls me into him. I instantly feel how much stronger he is than me.

He presses me up against the wall, his fingers grazing through fallen strands of my hair.

His eyes are determined.

He looks at me, letting a few seconds pass and then he kisses me. I can feel his belly pressing up against my body and his tongue easing its way into my mouth.

I'm so shocked that for a moment I do nothing, but then, I find myself kissing him back.

I fall into him.

I allow his big warm arms to hold me close.

I've needed this feeling for so long. Relief floods through my body.

I dip my head down, stopping the kiss and pressing my forehead into his chest.

God it feels good to be held.

He cuddles me close and kisses the top of my head.

As wrong as I know this is, selfishly I can't remember the last time something has felt so good.

CHAPTER 17

Setting up Black Swan on Bibiana's television was supposed to be a clue.

I underestimate just how stupid people are in this town, especially the fucking police.

A ballerina consumed with dance, struggling with her sanity!

A white swan. A black swan. Dissociative Identity Disorder.

Paranoid schizophrenia. That's the premise of the film.

It couldn't have been more obvious.

I gnaw at my knuckles with frustration. The need to scream at the top of my lungs is enormous.

Instead, I let the electrifying sound of Pyotr Ilyich Tchaikovsky's music from Swan Lake calm me down.

I've been playing it on repeat for the girls.

Dancing around them, twirling and whirling through the basement.

I still need to dig more graves outside. That stupid old couple had ended up in two of them.

I'd dragged their beaten bodies right to the edge and kicked them in without a second thought.

I had to do it, didn't I?

God that feeling! Hearing their dead weight hit the ground hard was so enjoyable.

I'd covered them up as quickly as I could. I'd even gone to the lengths of picking a few flowers to place on top of their graves.

I'm not all bad! They turned out to be special to me, surprisingly.
They were my first ever kills, after all.
I'll deal with the graves later, though.
First, I need to have some fun and ease up this tension.

I've set up a little gas hob in the centre of the room today and
brought down an old scratched up pan to cook on in celebration
of the change of season.
The snow on the mountaintops are turning to sludge and there's a
promise for warmer days to come.
I saunter up to the girls, still bound to their chairs. They look
dismal, grey.
I recoil at the sight of the girls foot.
The rotting flesh where her toe once was is crawling with
maggots. They are feeding off of her, moulting, festering.
Flies are swarming all around her. She is delirious.
I swat the flies away and grab her limp foot for closer inspection.
Drawing the knife out from my back pocket, I slide it across her
remaining toes. Her head is heavy as she shakes it at me,
pleading eyes blinking down at me.
I flick maggots onto the ground with the knife, the tip of the blade
searing right into the wound. She roars in agony but
Tchaikovsky's 'Dance of the Little Swans' is so loud no one can
hear her.
In one quick, fluid movement I slice the blade right through her
remaining toes. They fall to the floor like little kidney beans.
Now she will never dance again.
Now, she is useless. Pathetic.
The one thing she was good at in life besides being a whore, is
gone.
I scoop the toes up and head over to the frying pan.
There's a bottle of canola oil next to the hob. I pour a hearty lug
into the pan and turn on the heat. The blood on my hands is sticky
and thick.
The toes sizzle angrily as I drop them into the oil. I turn to look at
the girl, she's passed out in her chair.

The oil spits at my bare arms.

I unscrew a bottle of Two Oceans white wine and splash a bit into the pan to simmer.

I grind some salt and pepper into my concoction, the smell of cooking flesh filling the room. The sauce is a mixture of seasoning, wine and blood.

I deposit the meal onto a plastic plate and head to the CD player to turn down the music.

"Whose hungry?" I ask the whores, holding out the plate.

One of the girls throws up, sick leaking through the duct tape covering up her mouth. She has no choice but to swallow. She's crying hysterically.

She's one of the new girls. Verity. Collateral damage, really.

She wasn't one of my targets. To my knowledge she never did what the others did, but who knows at this rate. It is possible that some slipped through the cracks.

She's also not a dancer so she isn't a part of the Corpse de Ballet I'm creating.

Oh well. The more the merrier at this point.

"This is all there is for dinner tonight. Come on, eat up!" I push the toes right under her nose, ripping the tape off from around her mouth.

Vomit drips down her shivering body. When she still resists I roll my eyes.

I pick up one of the toes, hot pink chipped varnish still visible.

I yank her mouth open and shove the toe between her lips.

She convulses, dry heaving.

I slam my hand over her mouth so that she can't spit the toe out.

"Chew it," I whisper into her ear.

Her black braided hair still smells fresh and clean, like coconut.

I don't expect her to give in quite as easily as she does, but beneath my hand I feel her starting to chew.

She squirms as her teeth crunch through the tiny bones.

"Swallow," I warn her.

I watch as I see her throat move in an unwilling gulp.

My hands are slick with her vomit and blood.

"Good girl," I pat her on the head and wrap a new strip of duct tape around her face again before moving on to the next girl.
"Looks like there isn't enough her to feed everyone," I pout.
"Maybe it's time for someone else to contribute!" The blade is in my hand.
I walk around the room, looking at all of the girls one by one. Who to choose next?
I choose slowly, smiling down at the girl who knows what is about to come.
Bibiana.

CHAPTER 18

I am so lost in Cody's mouth that I barely register the scream.
A piercing shriek followed by a stampede of students charging
down the hall.
I blink up at Cody questioningly.
What is going on?
Britt hurtles into the room, tripping over herself in the process.
The sound she makes is a gargled wail, something guttural.
"Britt, what-" I start to say but she slams the door behind a bunch
of other students who topple over each other to get inside.
"Call for help!" someone begs, tears falling freely down their
face.
I watch as another student drops to the floor, rocking themselves
back and forth.
That's when I hear the gunshot.
Everyone screams in unison.
My eyes go wide.
Cody slams me to the ground and puts his finger to his lips.
He squeezes his eyes shut as he silently begs everyone to keep
quiet.
Everyone is trembling with fear.
There are so many thoughts flying through my head.
A school shooting. I'd heard of them. Seen the devastation they
cause on the television.
I never thought I'd be in the middle of one.
You never think it's going to happen to you though, do you?

I'm in so much shock that I actually feel numb.

This cannot be happening.

Cody slips his phone out from his pocket and dials the police.

The line is engaged. I can hear the droning beep, beep, beep crackling through his speakers.

"Everyone must be trying to call them," he whispers shakily when he tries again.

Students are tucked away into the corners of the room, barricading themselves behind desks and bookshelves.

There's another gunshot that echoes throughout the school hallway.

Everyone jumps in fright.

"Why is he doing this?" Britt sobs frantically.

"He?" I ask.

"Luke! Luke came in with a gun. He started shouting at everyone. He told everyone they've made him do this," her shoulders are heaving up and down as she cries. She's clutching at her shirt, her fingers almost ripping it to shreds.

My stomach drops and for a moment, I'm sure I'm going to pass out.

Luke has a gun.

Luke is shooting in the school.

This is real.

What Chloe's dad said this morning comes flooding back to me.

'Luke took Chloe. I know he did. I told her from the start that boy was trouble. I swear I'm going to kill that son of a bitch myself.'

This is happening right now.

As hard as I try, it just won't sink in.

"He fucking killed all those girls and now he's here for us!" someone in the back yelps.

Cody grips my hand to ease the trembling.

His skin is clammy. Cold.

The glass of the schoolrooms door is frosted, but I can just make out a shadowy figure lurching towards us from outside. I can see without a shadow of a doubt that it's Luke's silhouette.

I can see the pistol he has in his hands.

He's resting his head against the glass now, hovering just outside the door.

We're all holding in a collective breath, silent in wait.

The gun taps against the glass, tantalizing us.

I look around the classroom. Cody and I are supposed to be the strong ones here.

We are the mentors.

It is our job to protect and look after these students, but we are just as petrified as they are.

"Ms. Brady..." Luke's voice shatters the silence.

"Knock, knock," he taps at the glass with the barrel of the gun.

Cody scoops me closer to him, holding me close.

The other students don't move a muscle. Their eyes are huge with fear.

"You need to tell them Ms. Brady. You're the only one who knows the truth," he sounds hysterical. His voice is quaking, high-pitched.

The doorknob starts to twist and with that Britt screeches into action.

"Stay the fuck away!" she cries, scrunching herself up into an impossibly tight ball. As if that would somehow save her.

"No, Britt. You don't understand!" I can see his body crippling over from behind the glass.

"You have to believe me. I didn't do anything to all those girls!" he sniffles.

"You're fucking crazy!" another student yells back.

I clench my jaw, wishing everyone would just shut up. Shut the fuck up! Don't provoke him.

We don't know how close he is to the edge.

"I'm not fucking crazy!" Luke bellows in rage, his fist pummelling into the glass. It doesn't break at first, instead a web of cracks instantly appears.

When he punches it again, shards of glass come flying into the room and everyone starts to scream.

"You want to play this game? Let's play," he spits.

Most of the students have their hands over their eyes.

127

"Look at me!" Luke begs everyone as he stumbles into the room.
His eyes seek me out.

He chokes on his saliva and bites back tears.

There's blood spatters on his shirt.

What have you done?

"Tell them, Piper!" he shouts.

I know he wants me to tell everyone about the threats.

To make them see he isn't involved in the disappearances, but I'm suddenly not so sure.

What if he made it all up?

What if he created these threats to make me trust him?

"Fuck!" his voice travels down the hallway.

He's infuriated with my silence. So am I, but I can't find my voice.

He kicks over my teachers desk, sending books, stationary and my sisters potted plant flying.

"Put the gun down, Luke." Cody's voice is strong and authoritative.

"No! I didn't do this! You guys have ruined my fucking life! Do you know what it's like? For everyone to look at you like you're a murderer? To walk by and hear people whispering and pointing?! You don't understand what you've done to me!" he's scratching the gun against his head.

His finger is on the trigger.

"I loved you," Britt is sobbing.

My head jerks in her direction.

Britt was seeing him too?

"No you fucking didn't! You turned your back on me just like every single one of you," he waves the gun wildly around the room.

The students are trembling behind upturned desks and shelving.

"I can't take it any more," Luke's bottom lip wobbles uncontrollably.

"You're a monster!" someone screams from behind me.

Luke snarls at him, he looks like an animal as he stalks right up to him.

The blast from the gun is deafening.

Everyone screams in unison as the body of one of my students falls to the floor, blood instantly pooling around him.

I make myself look.

It's Steve, one of Luke's best friends.

He's choking, clutching onto his stomach in sheer agony.

He's struggling to breathe.

I don't know how he's still alive.

I crawl on my hands and knees over to the boy. Putting my hand over the wound in the boys stomach, I start to apply pressure.

Thick, warm blood covers my hands.

It's slippery and I feel myself starting to slip.

I can't keep the pressure on, my arms feel like jelly.

Luke is staring down at us, his eyes look bizarrely glazed over.

He doesn't know what he's doing or what he's done. He can't.

There's no recognition as he looks down at his best friend, bleeding out at his feet.

Steve starts to cough, his blood spraying onto my face. He's dying in my arms.

We all stay silent as he struggles to take his last breath.

"No!" someone wails, but their cries are cut short with another explosion from the gun.

Another student falls right at my feet. A bullet to the head.

"Luke," I whisper, taking my hands away from Steve's lifeless body.

I can hear sirens getting closer to the school.

It's almost over.

Luke is standing over me, pointing the gun right at me.

"Please," I beg, holding my bloodied hands above my head. I can feel Steve's blood running up my arms, soaking my shirt.

"Don't do this," Cody pleads, very carefully edging closer to me.

I can't believe he's moving. He could be killed.

In that moment, I think I may love him.

"There's only one bullet left," Luke's voice is little more than a murmur, but it's a warning.

Cody's fingers find mine.

Out the schoolroom window I catch sight of the flashing lights from ambulances and police cars.

It will all be over soon, I think, squeezing Cody's hand. The gun is still pointed at my head.

The sound of the squad running through the hallway echoes into the room.

I can hear them kicking other classroom doors open, trying to find us.

"Fuck," Luke quivers, the panic in his eyes unmissable now.

He knows they're coming for him.

He brings the gun to the side of his head.

Cody's grip on my arm tightens. We're both relieved that the gun is away from me at last but petrified at what he is going to do next.

"I didn't do it. I didn't take those girls," his voice breaks.

They are his final words.

He cocks the gun, looking right at me.

Every memory I have with him from our short time together flashes before my eyes.

I stare back at him, shaking my head, silently begging him not to do this.

I can't tear my eyes away, until they are blinded by blood.

*

Shards of Luke's skull are stuck to my clothing, poking through the material and digging into my skin.

Little bits of bone have entangled themselves into my hair.

I'm waiting for detective Engelbrecht to come back into the room.

I'm becoming *really* well acquainted with him now.

He needs to ask me more questions.

I'm only here to make a statement, but it feels oddly like an interrogation.

We had to take a break. The sight of Luke's head exploding has permanently embedded itself into my brain.

It happened so fast. In the blink of an eye, his face was gone. Destroyed.

"I should have said whatever it took to calm him down, but I didn't. I killed him," I cried as he pushed a mug of tea in front of me.

He looks tired, unsympathetic, like he always does.

I can tell he's unsurprised to see me surrounded by all of the drama once again. At least this time, I'm sober.

He didn't just watch someone's brains splatter against the wall.

He's just doing his job. Come five o'clock he'll head on home and switch off, push whatever slivers of information about a suicide and a school shooting he had to note down far from his thoughts.

How I wish I could be him; but I will never forget.

When he's certain I've detailed everything I can possibly remember, he lets me go.

I step out into the chilly afternoon fog that hovers heavily across the entire town and head towards my car.

Everything that happened before Luke shot himself is hazy, but I find myself thinking about what Britt had said.

She'd told him she'd loved him.

How had he managed to juggle us all this way?

Hadn't Britt known about Bibiana, anyway?

Out of everyone, he'd been most public about his relationship with Bibiana.

I'm chewing the inside of my cheek, trying to wrap my head around it. Both Bibiana and Chloe were seeing Luke and now they were both missing.

I'd been seeing Luke and had been getting threats.

A thought occurs to me.

Could Bibiana and Chloe have been getting threats too?

If so, why hadn't they come forward about it?

Nothing makes any sense, it's making the pounding in my head worse and worse.

I scrunch up my eyes and massage my forehead, wishing I had more pills on me.

I'm desperate for a shower. To change into fresh clothes and wash the clumps of blood from my hair. To take my pills and sleep. Exhaustion is taking over.

Cody had wanted us to be together tonight after everything that happened today, but I'm just not up to it.

I'm a few meters away from my car when a flash obscures my vision. I'm momentarily blinded.

I stumble forward, gripping onto the trunk of a tree in front of me for support.

I shake my head and open my eyes.

A searing headache almost makes me want to scream. It's unbearable.

I close my eyes again and instantly a flash of an image is in my head.

It scares me.

I can't make it out at first. I don't know what is happening. Everything is all blurry and too bright.

I concentrate hard, willing the image to focus.

The figure of a girl getting into a car slowly emerges.

The engine revs to life.

The girl adjusts the rear view mirror and investigates her eye make-up for a few moments.

I open my eyes again and blink several times.

The streets are quiet. I whirl around at the sound of a car engine starting up.

It's the same car I had just seen in my head.

I don't understand what is happening to me.

How had I seen that?

I squint to see who the driver is. She's brushing mascara onto her lashes. When she puts the tube of mascara away I can see her clearly.

It's Britt.

She fans at her eyelashes for a few moments to let them dry before indicating.

She turns out of her parking space.

I watch in stunned silence as she starts to drive away.

There's the sound of another car starting up just up the street.

They're further away so I can't make out who is behind the wheel at all.

They too pull out of their parking space and creep forwards in the same direction as Britt, who has stopped at a stop street just up ahead.

I'm well hidden behind the tree I'm still holding on to so neither driver notices me.

As the driver in the car behind Britt edges past me I notice that the driver is wearing a big, black hoodie.

It's impossible to make out who it is, but I'm suddenly absolutely convinced that they are following Britt.

She's in danger.

I sprint towards my car and yank at the seatbelt as I put my keys into the ignition. I have to follow them.

I'm busy trying to unlock my phone but I'm shaking so much that I keep getting the password pattern wrong.

I look up and see Britt and the car behind her starting to move again.

There is no time to call the police right now.

I can't lose them.

I discard my phone, tossing it onto the passenger seat.

Gripping the steering wheel with sweaty hands, I start to follow them. All thoughts of my shower and sleep forgotten.

I try to keep a good distance to not attract attention.

When Britt turns down a road to the right, the driver behind does the same.

I'm not being paranoid, whoever is in that car is definitely following her.

I speed up slightly, worried I'll lose them once they've rounded the bend.

I forget to indicate as I swerve down the street they'd taken and a car behind me hoots angrily. I look back at them and mouth an apology, the person in the car is shouting at me and waving their hands around. I don't have time for niceties.

I look back towards the road in front of me and my heart leaps into my throat. Up ahead is a roundabout with three different exits.

I have no idea which one they've taken.

Frustration takes hold.

I'm about to pull over and call the cops when another flash comes.

My eyebrows scrunch together in agony as I try to make out what the picture in my head is.

I'm about to burst into tears when I make out a street sign, covered in ivy but the wording is just visible. Elm street.

The picture in my head starts to move.

I'm in a car, but it isn't mine.

Gloved hands are at the wheel.

Up ahead I see Britt's car with her personalised plates.

In my head I'm following her and I feel a sickening thrill for it, an anticipation of what's to come.

In my head, I want to hurt her. Torture her. Make her pay.

I open my eyes and I'm back in my car, in front of the roundabout.

My entire body is trembling with fear and confusion.

I scan each turn off for a street name.

Everything around here is so overgrown and old.

I see the ivy before I see the sign. It looks exactly like it did in my head. The faded lettering on the street sign reads, Elm Street.

I have absolutely no idea what is happening to me; why I am seeing things in my head and why I am feeling these things.

It's bizarre and overwhelming but I have no choice other than to press my foot down on the gas pedal.

I take the turning onto Elm Street.

It's a street full of red bricked, double storied homes with gable rooftops.

I rub at my eyes as I explore the area, looking for any sign of life.

It's only midday so most people will still be at work, though it still feels eerily quiet.

There's no one milling around on the streets anymore.

Not since the Pirouette Predator surfaced.

All of the houses are identical.

I see a scruffy looking Yorkshire Terrier staring at the world outside from a window. He barks at my car as I drive by, a high-pitched yelp that could wake the entire neighbourhood, if anyone was home.

It makes me think of River.

Guilt immediately builds inside of me.

I'm momentarily lost in thought about my dog when I hear a car close by.

I snap back to reality and hunker down in my seat so that no one can see me. I peer just over my car window and see Britt exiting her car.

There are no other cars around to be seen.

She slings her handbag over her shoulder, looking all around her as she bolts up to a front door.

Before she gets there, the door swings open.

I hold my breath as I watch a middle-aged man wrap his arms around her.

A woman comes to the entrance too, her hand over her mouth as she shakes her head and sobs.

Britt is a mess.

She's crying and rambling words I can't hear from my car.

I recognise the couple she's with. I've seen them at the school before. Her parents.

She's safe. She's home.

A third flash comes, but this time it's a feeling instead of an image. It's a feeling of complete and utter anger.

It frightens me.

That fucking little slut! A voice comes out of no where.

It's in my head.

It's *my* voice.

I rake my fingers through my filthy hair and start pulling at it, trying to rip it from my scalp.

I want it to stop.

I want to make the voices stop.

I wait until the door to Britt's home closes behind them before I start up my engine and very slowly make my way back to the cottage.

While River does her business out in the garden, I swallow my medication with a big glass of water.
I stand under the shower for what feels like hours, my students' blood washing off of me and pooling on the tiles at my feet.
I watch as the water cascades down my naked body. My once tiny figure has changed so much these past few weeks.
I look seven months pregnant I'm so bloated at the moment.
My guess is that it's all the alcohol. It could also be the medication. I've heard anti-psychotics cause weight gain.
I wish I could stop taking them, but then I know how dangerous that could be.
God I miss my old body. It's painful to look in the mirror these days.
Michael used to tell me that I must have serious body dysmorphia. Just another condition to add to my collection.
He used to tell me I looked amazing, that is, until he started telling *her* that she looked amazing, of course.
I'd never told him about my struggle with eating disorders as a kid.
The truth was, I loved seeing my bones protruding from my collarbone and hips. I felt dainty and cute.
Now, that flat stomach feels enormous.
I know I'm not pregnant, though. Can't be. Never will be.
I've accepted that now, so really, I could just throw the birth control away.
I sluice my disgusting body with hot water, the sound of the gunshot still ringing violently in my head.
I change, tossing the clothes from earlier into the bin as I walk into every single room in the cottage.
I check every nook and cranny until I'm certain I'm alone.
I lock every door and window and feel the pills starting to kick in.
My eyes are already rolling into the back on my head by the time I collapse into bed.
I black out, holding onto River's warm body like a security

blanket.

The night is dreamless and I am grateful for the brief escape to nothingness.
However, when I wake up and turn my phone back on there are countless alerts that come through all at once.
Our teachers chat group is flooded with messages.
Links to various news stories covering the school shooting.
Photographs of the students whose lives were taken.
Someone had even put up a video of Luke as he took his own life.
I recoil at the sight of it.
How has this not been taken down yet?!
Before I report the video, I can't help but scroll down to read the comments. They are diabolical.
Anonymous people have written that he's gotten what he deserved.
One comment with over one hundred thumbs up read:
Good riddance to The Pirouette Predator!
I had to stop reading the comments when some people had started commenting things like, *'Justice has been served. May all the girls and Ms. Robyn Brady rest in peace.'*
I slam my phone down hard onto the bedside table. It cracks the screen.
My sister is *not* dead!
It's the first time I've seen the words 'rest in peace' and my sisters name in the same sentence.
It's too much to stomach.
I'm in a nightmare.
I've been stuck in this nightmare for months.
I bury my face into my pillow and pray to God to wake me up.
Let me wake up back in Michael's arms, to be back in my home and planning my wedding.
Let me go back to the way things were before absolutely everything fell apart.
Please. Please. Please!
But when I open my eyes again, I'm still here... and more

messages are continuously flooding into my inbox.

I unwillingly pick my phone back up.

There's speculation into Luke's mental health and his connection to the missing girls.

Over half the school faculty believe he is responsible for the abductions. Cody is among them.

He doesn't know what I know – and he never will.

No one will.

Some teachers are adamant that Luke, despite all of his faults, would never have done the things people are accusing him of.

There's a discussion about bullying and how to prevent it on campus.

One of the teachers, a woman I've never spoken to before, left the last message on the group that seems to have silenced people for now, at least.

It read:

'Luke was pushed to the breaking point by both his fellow students and his teachers. I do not for one second believe he had anything to do with being The Pirouette Predator. Ask yourself how you would feel if everyone was accusing you of something that awful. It's no wonder the poor boy went mad. I saw the way people were looking at him! Shame on all of us for not consoling him when he needed some support.'

I think back to yesterday, to what Luke had said.

"I didn't do it. I didn't take those girls."

They were the last words he ever spoke.

He maintained his innocence right to the very end.

The look in his eyes, that hopeless begging stare he'd given me before he pulled the trigger haunts me.

I desperately want to believe he was being truthful.

If he was innocent and he really was being threatened by someone else, then that person is still out there.

I think about the car I'd seen following Britt home, but I can't even remember the make or colour of it.

I'm starting to second guess myself.

When I'd finally found Britt, there had been no other cars out on the street that led straight to a dead end. Was there ever another car at all?

My mind is spinning, playing tricks on me.

Maybe I'm the one who was following her. Me and me alone – but why? I'd been so sure that she was in danger. I could literally sense someone's strong desire to hurt her and it felt riveting. Exciting.

Was it my desire?

I think about that envelope with the photographs of Luke and I inside it, how the handwriting looked like mine.

I think about the amount of tablets I've been taking lately, enough to make me have no recollection the next day.

It's all eating away at my brain.

I quickly shake the thought from my head.

It's impossible.

Someone *has* been threatening me.

Someone did unthinkable things to my dog.

Someone took my sister and all the girls from school.

Someone did something to that old couple out on their daily walk.

Someone is still out there.

CHAPTER 19

I hook River's leash onto her harness and she hops excitedly towards the front door, tongue lolling out the side of her mouth. I've bundled up in my big coat and wrapped a huge scarf around my neck.

It's colder today. The weather is toying with us.

I shiver as I walk down my sisters driveway, stopping every so often for River to sniff at tree stumps and plants.

It's rubbish day, so everyone's wheelie-bins are outside on the side of the road. I try to ignore the homeless people rummaging through them as I walk on by.

They're scattering litter everywhere, discarding empty packets into the road as they desperately search for something edible.

My neighbours rubbish tumbles down the lane in the morning breeze.

On the way to Luke's house, I stop off at the supermarket.

I pick out a bouquet of yellow flowers, the stems bound together with a white silk bow.

I can't even imagine how Luke's mother must be feeling right now. Word is that she arrived at the house after news of the shootings spread.

His house looks like it has been ripped apart.

Eggs have been thrown all over the outside walls and doors.

Rocks have been tossed through the windows.

Toilet paper has been flung all over the trees and roof.

My heart breaks for his mother the moment I see it.

There's a security man parked outside now to keep the harassment at bay, I guess.

He stops me as I'm opening up the gate to the entrance.

"I'm just here to drop these off. I was Luke's teacher," I tell him.

He eyes the bouquet suspiciously for a few moments before nodding me through.

I can feel his eyes on the back of my neck as I reach the front door.

My finger trembles as I press down on the bell. I grimace as I pull back and realise the bell is full of sticky egg yolk.

"Who is it?" a woman calls from behind the closed door.

She's pulled back the sheer curtain just a crack and is peeping through.

"Mrs. Archer, hi! It's Piper Brady, I am – *was*, Luke's teacher," I bite my lip at my choice of words.

There's silence for a few seconds.

She's dropped the curtain back down again so I can't quite tell if she's still there or if she's walked away.

"What do you want?" she asks some time later, her voice cold and vulnerable.

River pants at my legs, looking up at me with her big, warm eyes.

"I've – I've brought you some flowers," I call through.

It suddenly seems stupid now to have brought a woman who has just lost her son a bunch of cheap roses from a supermarket.

They are limp in my hand.

I'm starting to regret having come.

"I'll just leave them by the steps," I say, crouching to place them on the Welcome mat at my feet.

I'm walking back down the pathway wondering what the hell I was thinking when I hear the door unlocking.

It creaks open and the tiniest, red faced woman pokes her head out.

"Come in before those bastard children come back with more eggs," she shouts over to me.

Her paper thin hands give River a pat on the head as we enter the house.

141

Being back here is bizarre.

My stomach flips at the sight of the sofa, where Luke and I had once had sex.

It still feels like a nightmare.

How can he be dead?

"Tea?" his mother asks me as I follow her into the kitchen.

The curtains are all drawn closed and there's very little natural light getting in.

"Please. Just a bit of milk and no sugar," I say.

"Afraid I've only got this soy milk, that alright?" she shakes her head, her eyes welling up.

"Perfect," I give her a weak smile, watching her pour the milk into our mugs.

"Luke told me he was going to go vegan or something before – you know..." her voice trails off.

I'm reminded of that very first time I visited Luke here, when I'd snooped around and found an old lamb knuckle in his fridge.

I can't imagine him turning vegan.

"He said it was good for your health or some nonsense. Told me to watch this documentary on Netflix called The Game Changers. He had plans, that boy. I can't believe he's gone," her shoulders heave as she lets out a sob.

My hand instinctively reaches out to comfort her.

When I do, she falls into me like she's been desperately needing support.

"Who buys a big carton of milk if they're going to – if they're going to-" she can't finish the sentence.

"I'm so sorry," I whisper into her ear.

She has a musky smell on her skin that I breathe in as I rock her back and forth. It's strangely intimate considering I've only just met her, but it feels like the right thing to do.

I can sense the relief in her as her entire body lets go and just cries.

I know the feeling all too well.

I have no idea what to say.

It would be stupid to ask her if she's okay.

Why am I here?

River is investigating all the new smells around the house, cautiously making her way down the hallway to the bedroom.

I remember Luke telling me that his mother had bought him those two hideous floral pillows as a house-warming gift a while back. She's clutching onto one of them now, cradling it in her lap like a baby.

"Luke told me you got those for him," I smile.

She instantly frowns at me.

It takes a moment for me to register what I've just done.

Time seems frozen in place.

Her body has gone rigid and I wonder how I'm going to explain this.

"You've been here before?" she asks me, slowly lifting her eyes up to meet mine.

I swallow hard, my eyes darting wildly around the room.

"Just how well did you know my son, Ms. Brady?" she crosses her legs, straightening up.

"I- well," I stammer.

Her eyes are unblinking.

"I dropped some homework off for him a while ago when he was sick," I lie, but it sounds completely unconvincing.

She purses her lips and cocks her head to the side.

"Why exactly are you here?" she asks.

"I just – I know Luke's been getting a lot of... hate..." I wince at the word.

She nods at me in agreement.

"I can't imagine what it must be like; and the students vandalising the house and saying all these things about him, it must be awful." My sincerity here, is obvious.

Her look softens slightly.

"It's only been a day and I just – I wanted to help somehow," I'm speaking but I have absolutely no idea what I'm saying.

"Help?" she asks, perplexed.

The image of Luke pulling the trigger flashes before my eyes.

There was so much blood.

Watching his lifeless body crumple to the floor, it makes me want to throw up.

Bile rises in my throat.

I'm hot suddenly and my heartbeat quickens.

I want my tablets. I'd taken two this morning already but it's not enough.

I can feel it coming on again.

A hellish panic, a complete blackout.

Not here. Not now.

"I'm grateful for the concern, dear," she sips at her tea, her voice snapping me back into the present moment.

I fight for my composure.

Her eyes have glossed over.

There's so much of Luke in her, even the body language is similar.

In that moment she looks so small and vulnerable.

The front door barges open and a man's voice booms through the house.

"Those fucking brats are going to get my fist up their asses if they come back. The front of the house is fucked!"

He comes stomping into the room and stops dead at the sight of me on the sofa.

I instantly know it's Luke's dad. The same height and build, the same jawline and lips.

This is what Luke would have grown into, a very attractive man.

"Who is this?" he asks Luke's mum, not greeting me at all.

His eyes are red and swollen.

In his arm he's got a cardboard box full of beer.

Luke's mum swallows nervously and places her mug onto the coffee table in front of us.

"This is – was, Luke's teacher," she's picking at the thread on the floral pillowcase.

"I'm in no mood for company right now," he huffs, big boots marching right past me and down the hallway.

He reminds me of one of my foster fathers.

Anxiety climbs up my back.

I clench my fists, trying to slow my racing heart.

I don't want to think of him.

"Get the fuck out!" I hear him bellow.

At first I think he's saying it to me, but then I see River bolt as fast as she can out of a bedroom, tail between her legs. She's shaking in fright, burrowing under my legs for protection.

"I think it's time for me to leave," I start to gather up my handbag and River's leash.

It's then that something catches my eye.

A book. One that looks all too familiar.

"Where did you get this?" I ask her, picking up Robyn's journal.

Luke's mother looks at it, puzzled.

"Huh, didn't notice that before," her eyebrows knit together as she watches me turn it over in my hands.

I need it.

What can I say, though?

I can't tell her that it's mine.

She'd wonder what Luke had been doing with it. But what if she looks inside it and realises that it's Robyn's?

She'll take it straight to the police.

The sound of a can of beer opening comes from down the hallway.

A part of me doesn't want to leave this tiny woman alone with him.

She's twisting her wedding band around on her ring finger.

I place the book down and try not to look desperate to have it.

She walks with me to the front door in silence.

I thank her for the tea and am just about to leave when I pat at my jeans.

"Oh shoot, I think I left my house keys inside. Let me just pop in and get them!" I hand her River's leash and rush back inside.

I'm thankful that she stays by the front door with River at her side.

My handbag is just big enough to squeeze the book inside.

I clutch it protectively to my chest as I say goodbye.

I'm half way down the garden path when she speaks again.

"I may not be the sharpest tool in the shed, Ms. Brady, but I know my son. He has never taken a sick day from that school. Ever. I understand you're relatively new there, but I'm telling you now, if you're in any way responsible for my son's suicide," her voice is clipped.

She pauses for a moment to let the word 'suicide' sink in.

"I will find out."

Her words shock me.

I have no response.

I stand there rooted to the spot in silence.

I shouldn't have come here.

Stupid. Stupid. Stupid.

The words swirl in my head.

I'm getting dizzy again. It feels as though I have vertigo. The world around me is spinning madly.

The security guard is leaning on the bonnet of his car, watching me carefully. Sussing me out.

I struggle to find my balance as I turn on my heels and leave the property.

I don't say a word to the security guard.

I keep my head down as I stumble past him.

As soon as I've rounded the corner, the world goes black.

*

CHAPTER 20

I am beside myself. Howling and sobbing on my hands and knees.
I'm in the centre of the circle, surrounded by the whores.
This was not supposed to happen.
I thought he was stronger than this.
How could he kill himself? How?!
We were supposed to be together. He was my everything.
My future!
My entire plan has fallen apart.
Everything has been for nothing.
My heart is broken.
I've never experienced pain like this. Never.
Not even when the fucker cheated on me. This is worse.
So much worse.
Cheating is forgiveable with enough grovelling and believe me
he'd need to do a lot of that if he'd stuck around!
Britt, too!?
How many of these girls are there?!
More and more keep popping up like relentless fucking weeds.
Regardless, I could have gotten over the cheating – but not this.
This has broken me... and who said psychopaths have no
emotions?
The girls are all staring down at me in astonishment.

They're startled, not used to seeing me like this.
I miss him already.
There's no chance of a funeral with an open casket viewing after what he's done to himself.
I'll never see him again.
I want to go to the morgue and find his body, hold him one last time before he starts to decay.
I want to breathe him in before the rank smell of death takes over.
Touch his hands while they're still warm.
I love him so much – but I'm so fucking angry at him.
The fury is taking over.
"Stop staring at me!" I gasp, screeching at the top of my lungs.
The girls' eyes are huge with fear.
They have no idea what has happened.
"Luke!" I wail, unable to contain myself.
I haven't cried like this in so many years. Not since I stood scared and helplessly as that man molested me.
I fucking hate men.
Rage and pure heartbreak consumes me.
I cannot breathe.

I have to release my anger. Luke has absolutely shattered me.
I want to hurt him as badly as he's hurt me, even though I know he's dead.
I know I'm not thinking logically, but I can't stop.
I think long and hard, lying on my back in front of the whores.
They watch me agonize over him for hours, crying and screaming and ripping my own hair out.
I have bald patches now.
No wonder Luke didn't want me.
I am pathetic.
Disgusting.
The stress from the past few weeks is all too much for me.
I am deteriorating just as quickly as the girls surrounding me.
When I look at myself in the mirror I don't even recognise myself anymore.

The dark rings beneath my eyes are deep and unforgiving.
My nails are bitten right down to the quick.
My skin is dry and flaking and my body losing all muscle.
I have truly let myself go.
It is all Luke's fault.
He did this to me.
I used to be strong but little by little he tore me to shreds. I didn't
even notice it at first.
I suppose there were always subtle clues. His phone would ping
while we were together, hidden away from the world. No one
could ever know about us. I was his dirty little secret.
I'd stroke my fingers through his chest hair and ask him who was
messaging him so late.
'No one important,' he'd always say. I had loved that answer.
The naivety of it infuriates me.
I thought I was so special with that answer. It implied that I was
important. Better than everyone else!
Lies. All lies.
I used to have a fridge magnet that said, 'Sometimes I feel like a
mushroom. I'm kept in the dark and fed with bullshit.'
That is exactly what Luke had done with me.
He hadn't wanted anyone to find out about us.
He hadn't really wanted anyone to find out about any of his other
relationships either, apparently.
Besides fucking Bibiana.
She was always a bit more special than the rest of us.
More public.
I pick my wasted body up from off of the floor and lurch towards
her now, my eyes venomous.
"I don't know what he saw in you."
My lips curl up into a cruel grin. I squeeze her mutilated foot in
my hand, dried blood flaking off.
Warm fresh blood pours out as I tighten my grip. She screams
until the duck tape loosens around her mouth.
It's a piercing screech, her eyes filled with tears.
I slap my bloody hand over her mouth to silence her.

149

"Shh," I coo.

She's still trying to scream, but I can feel her weakening.

I start to sing to her.

Hush Little Baby.

That always used to help me calm down as a kid, when I woke up from the nightmares.

It works like magic. After a while her eyelids start flickering.

I look at her pretty little face, examining it closely.

She is no better than me.

She hid behind so much make-up every day.

It was all an illusion. Contouring, enhancing her best features...

She's a manipulator.

Without it all, she is nothing. A nobody. Like me.

I'm still pondering over why she was the lucky one who got more from Luke than anyone else when it comes to me.

The sun is setting in the sky and I realise what my next step is.

His fucking parents. They're here.

I am bloodthirsty.

I lick my lips, they're cracked and chewed open from my torment.

The girls haven't eaten properly for a day or two, maybe three.

I lose track of the days, but I couldn't care less right now.

They can wait.

I grab my car keys off of the floor and sprint up the staircase.

This was never supposed to be how this went.

I didn't intentionally set out to actually kill people.

I just wanted to scare the girls away from Luke. Make them see that he was mine! But I guess I hadn't thought it through properly. When my mask had slipped down and they saw who I was, I knew I could never let them go.

As much as they begged and pleaded, their fate was sealed... and once I started hurting them, it started getting addictive. Fun.

But I want the world to know I hadn't actually killed anyone until that nosy old couple who stumbled across me digging some graves.

At that stage I wasn't sure what I was going to do, really.

You see, I had to kill them.

They would have gone straight to the police, I'm sure of it.
I couldn't have that... and that feeling of power that came over me
when I took their lives, it was unlike anything I'd ever felt
before... and now I need that adrenalin rush again.
I'm quivering with excitement.
I have renewed vigour.

Luke's mum and dad are next.
I'll deal with Britt later.

CHAPTER 21

They never even had the chance to bury their son.

Luke's home was apparently a bloodbath when the police kicked the door in after two days of no sign of life coming from within.

It was the security guard who had raised the alarm.

He had gotten used to seeing Luke's mother's shadow moving around in the window, making copious cups of tea.

The news-reporter's are saying that Luke's dad had gotten drunk, killed his wife with multiple stab wounds and then turned the knife onto himself.

That's how it was staged to look, in my opinion.

There is no doubt in my mind that they were murdered.

Killed by the same person who took those girls, who tormented Luke, who took River's leg and who has been playing with me this entire time.

It wasn't Luke. I know that now.

I wish I'd said that to his mother. I wish she'd had someone tell her they believe her son was a good person before she died.

She went to the grave thinking the entire world despised her son – and despised her for ever having him.

I should have said something.

Our meeting plays through in my mind, all the things I could have said or done.

I could have made a difference, but I didn't.

I offered her some shitty supermarket bought flowers.

I left her with suspicions.

I left her with an evident argument brewing with her husband.

Penitence stews inside of me as I think about the last few hours of her life.

I think it will haunt me forever.

That poor woman.

It sickens me how many people are relieved they are dead.

Social media has exploded.

Once again everyone has their own theory.

Photographs of Luke's vandalised house have gone viral.

Some say his dad went mad, others are saying the students who were trashing their house teamed together and killed them.

Only one thing seems pretty clear at this point. Everyone is in agreement that Luke was the killer and he is now gone.

Everyone but me.

Police are investigating his phone records, trying to track his movements from where his phone hit signal towers on the days leading up to his suicide.

Search parties have tripled in an effort to find all the missing girls, now deemed dead.

No one believes they'll be found alive at this stage.

I'm sitting on the floor, clutching onto a photograph of my sister.

She was one of those girls.

If what everyone's saying is true, then my sister is dead.

I don't know if I can carry on without her.

I kick the wall in front of me, letting the tears flow freely down my face.

River can sense my sadness and limps over to me.

She puts her head into my lap.

I've been sitting here for hours, paging through Robyn's journal.

It's brutal to read.

I know I haven't been the best sister over the years, but I had no idea just how much she was suffering.

Our childhoods in and out of foster homes definitely took its toll on us.

I wish I'd asked her from time to time how she was doing, but I never did.

I was always so excited to share my travel experiences with her that I never really gave her the chance to speak.

There are pages and pages of her writing about our past.

I have to put the book down after an hour because it's too hard to remember it all.

When I pick it back up, steaming mug of fennel tea in hand, I start reading massive chunks of entries about her relationship with Luke.

She, like me, had to be kept a secret and it doesn't look like she'd handled it well.

My sister was in deep.

She even had pencil sketches of his face on some of the pages.

I've never known my sister to be in love, so it cuts me deeply that she never told me about this.

Then again, she couldn't, could she?

I carry on reading until one entry really hits me hard.

I think Luke's gone to meet another girl out on his boat.
I can't help but imagine him right now, fucking her on the lagoon.
It sickens me.
I can't stand his lies anymore.
I feel so out of my depth.
I'm not in control of anything.
I wish he'd just tell me, it's not like we are officially together anyway. We can't be... not yet. But he doesn't tell me anything that would paint a bad picture of himself.
Instead, he always seems to focus on <u>my</u> flaws.
Before he left my place, he told me I live my life in fear.
He said that it controls me.
The fear of losing him.
The fear of being alone.
The fear of not having my happily-ever-after with marriage, kids and the cliché white-picket fence.
I know he's right, but it's infuriating that someone so young can say that to me, even if it is true.

He knows me better than I thought he did – and that scares me.
The thing is, I just don't know HOW to let life unfold naturally.
I wish I did.
I mean, it feels like I'm destroying my own life with my
desperation.
Even my sister is getting married.
Maybe that's it. Maybe I'm getting scared of being left behind.
Piper and I were supposed to do everything together.
We used to huddle in bed together and pinky promise each other
that one day we'd get married and have babies at exactly the
same time.
At my age I guess I'm stupid to have still been holding onto that
promise.
Today has honestly been the worst day of my entire life.
I've worked so hard to get over my depression... but the knife went
to my wrist like a magnet.
At least if he told me the truth about seeing other girls, I wouldn't
feel like he was outright lying to me.
Honesty would be so much better.
God I'm pathetic... listen to me! I'd rather be a pushover and let
him see other girls as long as he told me about it.
What has happened to me?!
I'm numb now. I still cry... but I feel like I'm hollowing out.
There's not much left for me to give.
He has no idea how he is making me feel. Like an annoying 'blob'
who just gets in the way.
This is actually worse than a physically abusive relationship.
I'd take that over this any day.
Fuck him.
FUCK HIM.
He's fake.
Why am I so stupid?
Why do I still love him?
He's an asshole with more emotional baggage than my sister and
I put together!
I want to scream.

I feel like I have to tiptoe around him.
I feel so unwelcome in his life until he gets horny and demands
my presence with his raging hard on.
He is breaking me.
I can only hold on for so much longer before I crack.
I swear to God if he is cheating on me....

Reading the entry, it had started out so neat in her pretty cursive writing; but as it went along the messier and more angry the words became.

I hate seeing how much she's been bottling up inside and struggling alone.

What happened to us? We used to be so close. Tell each other everything.

The entry makes me so angry at Luke for making my sister feel that way.

He made me feel that way too, the way she feels is uncanny to how I felt.

For the briefest of moments I am happy he's dead.

Having her journal in my hands makes me want to get mine out again. It's jammed into one of the boxes I came here with.

Maybe I should start writing again, I decide.

Maybe it will help me somehow through everything that's going on right now.

Writing used to be so therapeutic for us.

I continue to flip through the pages and after a while I notice a list. It takes me a moment to realise exactly what it is.

A list of girls.

The first few are all the girls who have been abducted, but there's others too.

The ink colour changes towards the end of the list, written later on with a different pen, I think.

Britt's name is there and just below it, underlined angrily, is *my* name. I touch the letters. The ink smudges.

This was written recently.

I drop the book, my heart thumping erratically in my chest.

I don't understand – or at least, I don't want to.

The phone rings and I look down at it, still in shock.

It's the police station.

"Hello?" I say, trying to mask the tremor in my voice.

"Ms. Brady, it's Detective Engelbrecht," I recognise his voice instantly.

"How can I help?" I ask, my voice clipped.

He just thinks I'm a drunk who likes drama.

He doesn't believe a word I say.

"Ms. Brady, I need you to listen to me very carefully. Lock every single door and window in your house right now. I'm on my way over to you."

My stomach drops.

"What's going on?" I ask him, scampering around the cottage and bolting every lock I can.

"The speaker I took from you that night was left in the evidence room. I went in there today and it's gone," he's speaking hurriedly. I can pick up the anxiety in his voice.

"Gone?"

I can't quite comprehend what he's trying to say.

"Someone took it and they left something in its place."

"Well what did they leave?"

Panic starts to rise inside of me.

"A note," he says.

"What the fuck does the note say?!" I shout at him, unable to contain myself any longer.

Why isn't he just telling me?

Spit it out.

"She's next..."

I almost drop the phone from my hand.

"Don't worry Piper, I'm on my way," he tells me, hanging up the call.

My breath is hitched in my throat.

Beads of sweat roll down the side of my temple.

I'm losing control again.

The room around me is spinning, objects start to blur.

My knees buckle as I black-out completely.

*

CHAPTER 22

Luke, Luke, Luke.
If I didn't hate you so much, my love, I might actually have shed a
tear when I heard what you did. But then through time, I have
discovered how weak you really are.
You men are all the same.
I trusted you.
You were the first man I'd ever really had faith in.
It's never been easy for me, not with the childhood I had.
Accepting that I would never be normal from a young age
definitely made things hard for me, but I stupidly thought you
were different.
Oh how wrong I was!

I guess initially I'd wanted us to end up together, after all of this.
However, through time, things changed.
The girls were a bunch of sluts who needed to be dealt with.
It took me a while to realise just what a slut you were too.
A man whore, as they say.
How had I been so blind, Luke?
How had you managed to pull the wool over my eyes the way that
you did?
You thought you were so clever. Top dog.

You thought you could get away with anything – but look where that got you! Six feet under.

I'm glad you're gone.

The world is better off without people like you.

Cheaters, liars... you're all the same and you deserve every inch of pain that has come you're way.

In a way, I've won.

Now the question is, where to from here? You've definitely put a little spanner in the works, my love.

You've always done that though, haven't you? Fucked things up right till the very end.

I bristle. A cold wind bites at my bare arms.

The bark on the tree I'm leaning against is damp, dew from the morning seeping into my shirt.

I suppose I'm out here trying to have a moment of silence for you, Luke.

Despite everything, I had thought we would work things out.

Run away together after you realized everything I've done, I've done for you... for us! And now you've left me! Ha! Just like everyone else.

Can't trust anyone anymore, can you?

I rake my bitten fingernails through my hair.

I need to come up with a new plan.

Do I continue with everything, see things through to the end? Or do I just give up as you did and come to find you in hell?

The truth is, I actually don't know if I want you anymore.

Not after what you've just done. Left me when you knew I was doing this for us!

You stupid prick.

You couldn't just wait.

Perhaps you never wanted me at all.

Was everything you ever told me a lie? Spewing words that didn't mean anything out of your mouth to me, like you did with all those sluts?

They're all down there now.

Fading away.

Their ribs are jutting out, almost piercing through their skin.
Stomachs bloated, skin ruined.
A thought strikes me.
I could just leave them. Let them slowly starve. The police will
find them eventually.
There are three stages of decomposition. Did you know that?
Stage one is Livor Mortis. That's when the body starts to turn a
purplish, bluish colour about thirty minutes after death.
Algor Mortis comes next. That's when the body goes cold.
The fascinating thing is that the skin, the bodies biggest organ, as
well as bones can stay alive for days after death, so I've heard!
But it takes about a twenty-four hours for a human body to be
completely cold after death.
The last stage of decomposition is Rigor Mortis.
I remember the first time I saw it. I was on a road-trip and this
horse was just lying in the middle of a roundabout. It must have
been hit by a car. It's legs were sticking right up in the air.
I couldn't look away.
In Rigor Mortis all the muscles in your body contract and stiffen
up. The body can stay that way for a good day or two.
That is how I want the police to find The Corpse de Ballet.
I have the costumes for it and everything!
The scene will look so beautiful. Maggots and flies will be feeding
from them.
I can picture it now...
It can't happen any later than that. If they aren't smart enough to
figure it out I'm going to have to plant more clues.
If I leave it too long, their bodies will start to liquify.
Their hair and teeth will start to fall out.
My scene will be ruined.
I can't have that.
I may have lost Luke, but this part of the plan has to play out the
way I see it in my head.
It is only a matter of time – and I know I need to make my next
move.
I hadn't quite expected it – but I'm having so much fun!

It's become a game. One I think I might just stick around for, even though you put a bullet between you're fucking eyes, Luke, my love.

I let a few more minutes pass me by as I pick at a scab on my ankle. I pinch the skin, forcing the fresh blood out. I let it trickle warmly down into my sock.
A helicopter is circling the woods overhead.
They're getting closer, as I knew they would.
I know they're looking for my girls.
I've had to cover up the old couples graves by scattering old rusted drums over them. Make it seem less conspicuous.
I was able to find big plastic sheets to lay over the tops of the open ones for now. I'm hoping the pilots won't get curious and send a search party here.
I think I've covered it all up as best I can.

I suppose it's time for me to tell them. Break the news.
I wonder how they'll react.
As different as we are, the one thing we all have in common is that we did actually love Luke. He had that way with women, you know? This power over us. Like a fucking Harry Potter love potion. But, just like good old Hermione says, it doesn't actually produce love.
No!
It produces infatuation... obsession.
I pick myself up from the sodden ground, keeping my eyes trained on the helicopter above as I make my way to the building. The whore house, I should say.
I circle the girls as I choose my words.
"I have something to tell you all," my head is held high.
I can't wait to see their faces. Break their hearts.
We can suffer through this together!
I suddenly feel like I am not alone. Yes, Luke, my darling, I hate you. But there's no denying that there is a little twinge in my heart! A subtle pang of pain remembering the days spent with

you.

How happy I was.

Knowing that will never be possible again does sting, just a little bit.

It's not like I'm going to cry or anything.

Oh no!

I will however be able feed off of their emotions. Feel their heartache.

It's how I'm supposed to feel, you see.

They aren't completely useless after all. They teach me how to act if someone asks me about Luke's death.

I can mimic them. I've always been good at that.

Perhaps they could even teach me a thing or two about empathy.

So really, having these sluts here is a marvellous thing.

"I suppose you're wondering why I have gathered you all here today," I try and sound professional, like a preacher, but I can't help stifling a laugh.

"It is with a heavy heart," I continue, my hand on my chest.

"That I must announce the passing of our beloved Luke Archer."

Bibiana hangs her head low and starts sobbing silently.

Some are staring at me angrily, others are blinking back the tears, shaking their heads.

"Have you all come to realise what you have in common, yet? Besides being dancers, I mean. You must see there's a reason you're all in this room together, surely?" I ask, looking each and every one of them in the eyes.

It's Chloe who tries to speak.

I saunter over to her and rip off the duct tape.

"Start to scream and I'll start slicing off your fingers," I warn her.

"We're all here because we were all with Luke?" she asks, her voice hoarse.

"Ding, ding, ding!" I pat her on the head as a reward.

"First guess, too! You are a smart little one aren't you?"

One of the other girls starts to thrash wildly, shaking her head at me with big wide eyes.

"Oh yes. Forgot about you. Sorry sweetheart. Collateral damage," I wink.

"Tell us, Verity, what does your name actually mean?" I already know the answer, but remove the tape from around her mouth and let her speak.

"It means, Truth," she whispers, staring at the ground.

"Exactly!" I say excitedly, jumping up and down.

This just keeps on getting better and better.

"And what was it you just said, Chloe?"

"That we've all been with Luke," she's crying now.

"All except you," I wiggle the knife in Verity's direction.

"I'm sorry you have to die because of all of these whores," I try to sound genuine but I fear I have failed.

"I didn't do anything. Please let me go. I won't tell anyone. I promise!" she begs me.

Bibiana looks at her in disbelief.

Oh the joys!

"Honey, I have no more trust in you than I do for these whores. Now, Bibiana. Tell me, how does it feel knowing all these girls, your so called 'friends,' were opening their legs for Luke behind your back while you were with him?" I want to see her angry, betrayed.

I need to see her emotions unfold, but she's not looking at me. She's just sobbing, mucous dripping down onto her shirt.

"Bibiana!" I scream, making all of the girls jump.

"Angry!" she cries, her voice echoing throughout the basement.

"That's it!" I can feel the adrenalin coursing through my body as I approach her.

"Who are you most angry at?" I want to make her choose, but she shakes her head in response.

I grip a handful of her hair and pull her close to me. Our noses are just about touching.

"If you don't choose right now, I'll hack off every inch of hair on your pathetic little head," I warn her.

She's trembling as she looks up at me, eyes full of hate.

Then she swivels and looks right at one of the girls.

"Her," she whispers.

The girls eyes are colossal. She knows Bibiana has just chosen her to be the first victim.

We're all about to watch her die.

It feels like my body is vibrating I have so much excitement inside of me.

"Good. Now, I am going to untie you Bibiana. I want you to do exactly as I say. If you don't, I will kill you. Do you understand me?"

She nods slowly, her chest heaving up and down.

This is the most fun I have had in days. I don't know how much longer I can contain myself.

"I want you to feel what it feels like. It's incredible!" I'm laughing hysterically as I remove the bindings on her wrists and ankles. Drool falls down my chin.

"Stand up," I tell her, my smile so big it hurts.

She can barely hold herself up.

It takes a while for her to find her footing.

"Now walk with me over to her. Think about how angry you are at her. She slept with your boyfriend. She lied to you, Bibiana," I'm whispering right into her ear.

She has to hold onto my arm for support as we walk. She became weak so quickly.

I am buzzing as we stand in front of the girl.

"Now take this knife and take your anger out on her. Slowly at first. Play with her. You'll like it! You'll see," I am so thrilled to be sharing my desires with someone. Allowing someone to understand me.

She's going to see how thrilling it is.

I won't be alone anymore.

I drop the knife into the palm of her hand, holding tightly onto her chin just in case. One wrong move and I'll snap her neck.

I know how. Google is a wonderful thing.

The girl in the seat in front of us is writhing away, trying her best to fight.

She knows she has no chance.

We all do.

There's a tremor in Bibiana's arm as she brings the knife closer to the girls face. I wonder if she's as excited as me.

"Draw the blade around her face," I tell her.

She does as I say, just tickling the girls skin.

"Press harder," my voice is austere.

The girl flinches as the tip of the blade breaks through the surface of skin on her cheek.

Bibiana's knees are shaking, as if she's about to collapse.

"Go down to her chin," I say, watching as the blade cuts right down the girls jawline.

She is clenching her teeth together, screaming in agony.

"Deeper!"

As I shout my instructions, Bibiana whirls around.

I realise I'd stupidly loosened my grip on her neck in all of my excitement.

She swings at me, knife in hand but I am easily able to block her.

She's limping towards me as I walk backwards, refusing to take my eyes off of her.

I hear a crash behind me and quickly whip my head around to look but it's too late. Verity managed to crash to the floor, still bound, but I trip over her and land hard on my back.

Fuck, fuck, fuck.

"You stupid girl!" I snarl, trying to scramble to my feet but there's a searing ache in my shoulder from where I had connected with the concrete.

Bibiana is standing right over me.

"No. You're the stupid one, Ms. Brady," she says before plunging the knife right into the side of my neck.

CHAPTER 23

I come around to the wails of an ambulance and a paramedic
rushing up to me.
I am on the floor of a basement, choking on my own blood.
It hurts.
My pulse is out of control.
My neck is throbbing.
The pain is unreal. I must be dreaming.
I don't understand. Where am I?
My vision is blurred but I blink until I can make out a bunch of
figures around me.
More paramedics are checking vitals on other people. Other girls.
The girls.
They've found them!
I can hardly believe it.
I try to smile, to look around for my sister – but I can't move.
I am paralysed.
The only thing I can feel is fear creeping up my spine.
The area is being cordoned off.
Criminalists and the homicide squad are on the scene.
Have people died? Nothing makes any sense.
My visions hazy, but I can see people dusting for fingerprints.
IV needles are being put into some of the girls arms.
The paramedic is applying pressure to my neck as I'm carried
outside on a stretcher. I don't know what is going on.
Crime scene investigators are peering down into what appears to

be open graves.

One of the girls is pointing at me, telling a police officer something but I can't make out any words. I want to call out to them. *Help me.*

My ears are ringing. The ambulance is blaring. Sirens are screaming all around me.

I try to swallow but it's impossible.

Someone is pointing a camera lens in my face. I'm blinded by the flash as I get hoisted up into the ambulance.

I look up at the paramedic, terror in my eyes. The way he is looking at me alarms me even more.

I can tell he doesn't think I'm going to make it.

How did I get here?

Who did this to me?

Was I abducted?

Why don't I remember anything?

I feel my body going cold.

I am so tired.

I try to fight it but eventually I let my eyes close.

There's a tumbling sensation.

I'm falling, weakening, letting go.

The sirens fade away as I give in to sleep.

*

Four Months Later

Karen, one of the carers is spooning some sort of vile mush into my mouth.
It's supposed to be mashed potatoes, I think.
I am wasting away. My muscles have deteriorated.
Another carer, Kenyon, is massaging my feet. I wish I could kick her, but I have no feeling left from my shoulders down.
The massaging helps to stimulate my nerves, apparently.
They do all sorts of pointless stuff to my body really.
None of it works. Not the massages or heat packs or silly 'exercises.'
My nerves and muscles have deserted me, just like everything and everyone else in life.
They aren't happy to be dealing with me.
No one ever is.
I'm the girl who abducted all of those girls.
I murdered an elderly couple who were out on a little stroll. I've learned their names now. Amanda and Casey. I think hearing their names was supposed to make me feel something for them. It didn't.
I'm the girl who drove Luke mad, made him shoot up the school.
I killed his parents out of spite.
I pretended to be my twin sister for months.
Yes, it was all me.
Why?
That's the most common question I get asked.
'Why not?' I'd responded with a little twinkle in my eye.
What's the point in trying to explain it to them?
They would never understand anyway. The need for revenge. The anger and the pain. The resentment and God-damned torture I was put through that led to this!
For years my sister stood idly by, watching as our foster father touched me.

She never helped.

Why me?

Maybe they could never tell us apart and they didn't know they were always only going after me.

Either way, I hated her there and then for never helping me.

I'd cry and I'd cry as our foster dad would whisper into my ear, telling me how he'd come find me and kill me if I ever told anyone about 'our little secret'.

I was petrified.

I kept my mouth shut for years.

Robyn would slink away into the shadows, pretending not to hear what was going on.

How could she do that to me?

That is where this side of me came from, I think, but more on that later.

There's so much to tell you.

I've gotten what I deserve, they say.

I have a fucking suppository up my ass for God's sake.

They say the likelihood of me ever walking again is slim but not impossible – but for now, I am a quadriplegic patient getting spoon fed shit and watching my organs fail me.

It is humiliating.

I'd rather be fucking dead.

Border Line Personality Disorder. That was my diagnoses as a child.

Oh how wrong they were.

Sometimes I wonder if they'd realised the misdiagnoses sooner, would any of this have happened?

You see, so really it is all their fault. The doctors and the nurses who told me I was something I wasn't.

Labelled me.

Medicated me.

It wasn't bipolar disorder at all!

After that fucking bitch stabbed me in the neck, I was in intensive care for a while. I was teetering on the edge of life and death for weeks – but, I've always been a fighter.

I never gave up.
At first, no one knew who I actually was.
Was I Robyn or Piper?
Fingerprints answered their questions, as I wasn't to be trusted of course and Robyn was in a coma.
When I was finally rested up enough and able to speak again, the questioning began.
Doctor after doctor picked at my brain. My beautifully chaotic mangled brain.
Diagnostic tests were done.
I was slid into a tiny little tube that reminded me of a morgue.
It's as scary as they say it is, being there.
I've never been one to suffer from claustrophobia but holy shit, that could break the bravest of people.
Magnetic resonance imaging was done and it felt like I was trapped in that little tube for hours while nosy doctors analysed images of what really was going on in my head.
The invasion was distressing, to say the least.
Combined with my childhood trauma, history of eating disorders, the blackouts and the sleeping problems... it all led the doctors to the same, complex conclusion.
Multiple personality disorder; or Dissociative Identity Disorder as others like to call it.
I was 'predisposed' to the condition, they say.
Fucking hooray.
One of my favorite true crime podcasts, My Favorite Murder, have a quote – well, they have loads of brilliant quotes actually.
Quotes like:
'Toxic masculinity ruins the party again.'
True. So very, very true.
'Stay sexy, don't get murdered.'
Ha!
'Here's the thing, fuck everyone.'
I do love that one.
But right now, I think my favorite must be:
'Talk about your trauma.'

Oops.
Guess I should have done that.

The doctors say there is no cure for what I have.
I go to psychotherapy, though. I have to talk about my childhood all the time now, something I used to avoid at all costs.
We have to find my 'triggers.'
What is it that sets me off?
They're picking me apart, diving into the darkest corners of my life.
I am in my own personal hell.

It took some time to even start piecing together what happened but through time, little bits were revealed.
Hypnotists, clairvoyants and psychics were all called in to help like a fucking cavalry.
I had a breakdown and somehow I created this other life, where I was my sister. Two other lives, really.
The truth is, Michael and I split up way before I had let people believe. I left for my home town sooner than I told anyone, but not as Piper. As Robyn.
Did I know this was happening?
No.
I swear to tell the truth, the whole truth and nothing but the truth so help me God!
I was completely unaware of what I was doing when I 'switched' to Robyn.
There wasn't just one 'Robyn' either.
Oh no.
Somehow I created one version of Robyn who still loved Luke... whereas the other hated him for all he was worth.
The girls I'd abducted were able to tell police officers and social media all about my seemingly 'split personality.'
They told everyone how I went down there to the basement in hysterics one moment – then left for just a few minutes before coming back and being completely different.

No longer sad and howling over my loss of Luke, but actually laughing about it.

I can just imagine the stories swirling around the newspapers now. My face all over the front pages. Ridiculed.

Funny thing is, people in this town always used to warn potential boyfriends about me back in the day.

'Stay away from her,' they'd say.

'Trouble,' they called me.

I never really understood why.

I guess that's why I always wanted to get away from this wretched small town.

I needed to go somewhere new, where no one knew my name.

I needed a fresh start. No judgement.

When I left, I was able to bury my past. Forget about it.

I was no longer the girl who had grown up getting hurled in and out of foster homes.

I was free to be someone new.

Someone amazing.

I could breathe!

Anyway – I'm getting ahead of myself now.

Where was I?

Oh yes!

The adrenalin was incredible when I surprised my sister on her doorstep; and she looked so thrilled to see me.

She had no idea what was coming, how much I hated her.

We drank a bottle of wine out on her porch and caught up.

That's when she'd told me about Luke. It piqued my interest right away!

Luke added a new layer to the story – a layer I so desperately wanted and needed. It was a surprising little perk in my master plan.

When she finally needed the bathroom I slipped Rohypnol into her glass, all the while anger was bubbling up inside of me.

I despised her.

I watched the pill dissolve into the Chardonnay, feeling my excitement starting to grow.

I had to hide my smile when she came back outside and took a big sip from the glass.

The potency of the drug was amazing!

It's not something I'd ever used before, obviously, or even really researched. I had no idea how quickly it would take effect.

I guess that was the moment it really hit me.

This was happening.

It wasn't just some bizarre idea in my head anymore.

I was a bundle of nerves and excitement rolled into one.

Funny thing is, now that I think of it, the Rohypnol paralysed my sister completely.

At least she felt what I feel like now before I took her to that basement.

She was the first girl to be taken down there. She was still completely motionless when I tied her up to the chair, but she watched me all the while, her eyes blinking in confusion.

When the drug finally wore off she couldn't remember any of it.

"Why?" she had asked me, her face full of confusion as she struggled with her bindings.

"I want your life," I'd shrugged coldly.

"I don't understand, Pip. How can you do this to me? I'm your sister! I love you!" her voice was raising too much.

I was new to this, nervous of someone hearing her scream.

I slapped the duct tape over her mouth to quell her noise.

"Love me!?" I had laughed hysterically at that, I remember.

"Where were you when all that shit was going on when we were kids, Rob!? Tell me that. Nothing bad ever happened to you, did it!? You never helped me when I needed you the most. And you know what? Michael left me. You didn't know that, did you?!" I spat at her viciously.

She'd shaken her head at me then, her tears dropping down onto her lap.

"I can't do it all again, Rob. Don't you see how tiring it is to have to restart? But now, I don't have to. I can just take your life! It's genius, really. I honestly can't wait to meet Luke! He sounds

delightful," my eyes shimmered with excitement as my brain was still processing all of this information itself.

I started writing in the journal as her.
I even hid my car away for a while. It was when I finally parked it in the driveway and Cody noticed that everything started to really kick off.
I continued her scandalous relationship with Luke.
At first it was just supposed to be a bit of fun. I revelled in the idea of having a Toy Boy. But truthfully, I was desperate for love and I wanted Luke to see me, Piper, not Robyn anymore.
I'd lost Michael, but I had a chance now to have a ready formed relationship with my sisters lover. He would be none the wiser, and it worked!
I guess you can say I developed a bit of an attachment to him.
I was far too scared to lose him, the way I'd lost Michael. So when I started finding out that he was cheating on me, I may have lost it just a little bit.
Like I said before, men are all the same.
I, me, Piper, was a bit greedy when it came to Cody – but 'Robyn' didn't know about Cody.
'Robyn' saw Cody through Piper's eyes.
Are you keeping up? Just in case you're not, let me try to explain this to you.
Piper believed she got to town and that her sister was missing.
Piper started up a steamy romance with Luke completely on her own AND she still strung Cody along too. Slut.
'Robyn One' loved only Luke and 'Robyn Two' hated Luke.
When I became Robyn, I was disgusted at Piper for doing anything with Cody.
Of all people, really!?
Standards, darling. But I couldn't control that.
My dissociative disorder made me feel like I was watching Piper – like a fantasy.
I'd always had such a brilliant imagination as a kid. I made up so many imaginary friends.

So, when the doctors told me I'd developed this fantasy of truly believing I was watching Piper when I switched to 'Robyn,' it didn't really surprise me.

Luke was the only one who came close to discovering the truth. All that stuff on his computers search history was all because he suspected me.

He was trying to find out how many characteristics I shared with sociopaths.

He was researching psychopaths, trying to find out how common it is for a woman to be one.

I am neither a sociopath nor a psychopath.

I am also not a narcissist.

You see, those people can't love at all. I, however, do.

People misunderstand me completely.

People don't understand Dissociative Identity Disorder at all.

As hard as I tried to warn Luke, he just kept on digging.

He broke so much faster than I thought he would.

Why couldn't he have seen that I just needed him to stop his silly investigations?

He could still be alive today. Perhaps we could have even been together, but what's the point in thinking of what could have been now, right?

I'm sure in time, my heart will heal, the way it always does.

Time heals all wounds, they say. I say they just have to fester a little bit first; and fester, they did.

All those things I did to Piper, well, to me really, I was doing to myself.

I was planting cameras around the house and the speaker, too.

I was hiding the keys. Writing threatening notes to myself. Even talking to myself.

I was playing with myself, without even realising it! Making myself paranoid.

That's the fascinating thing about mental health disorders – they're actually pretty phenomenal, when you think about it.

Suddenly, the impossible is possible.

Crazy ideas become tangible and we don't even know it!
I was doing the most marvellous, seemingly implausible stuff
without realising it.
The truth is, I am capable of so much more than you.
I am power.
OK, well, 'Robyn' is.
I am merely their host.
It was explained to me that a 'host' is rarely aware of the other
personalities residing inside of them.
That's how I could SEE Piper, but she couldn't see me.
See that 'switch' I just did there?
It's so easy now, to take over whenever I want to.
I am in control.

Sneaking into the police station and into the evidence room was
easier than I could believe.
This country has seriously slack security. If there's something I've
learned, it's how easily people can be distracted.
When the officer went hurtling over to my sisters cottage thinking
I was in danger, I guess that's when I 'switched,' because when he
got there, the place was empty.
I've heard stories about what happened after I got stabbed.
Rumours circulate all around me every single day.
It isn't fair really.
That, you see, is where I am not in control.
You never can control what people will say about you behind your
back though, can you?
It's hard to let that go.
It's hard to know that people will come to their own conclusions
no matter what I say.
Anyway, after I got stabbed, Bibiana managed to untie one of the
other girls who still had all of her fingers and toes. She was sent
charging out of the basement in search of help.
She must have been running for quite some time before someone
found her. There's nothing close-by within walking distance where
I kept them. That's why what happened to that old couple is so

177

unfortunate.

They were just in the wrong place, at the wrong time.

In the state she was in it couldn't have been an easy journey. But she'd persevered and well, the rest is history.

I lost.

Game over.

K.O.

I know you must still have questions. I'm trying to get through them all.

I suppose one of the biggies is, what about River?! Everyone is always so concerned about the outcome of an animal in a story.

Dogs are so much easier to love than humans, aren't they?

Yes – yes, I did saw off my own dogs leg.

Do I feel good about it?

No! Of course I don't.

But you see the thing is, I wasn't in control!

There's certain things I still don't remember fully. Sawing off her leg being one of them.

I think the hypnotist decided to spare me there. I can only imagine it being the most horrific thing to see or do.

One thing does puzzle me, though. River still treated me with such love and adoration, every single day. Even after what I did to her.

We don't give dogs nearly enough credit, do we?

They can sense if a person is good or bad.

They can smell fear radiating off of us like a wretched stench.

Did she know it wasn't really me doing that to her?

She must have, right?

Otherwise surely she'd have turned on me!

She knew it was 'someone else' hurting her!

I AM innocent.

Regardless of that fact, my reputation is now tarnished. Although that sounds like a bit of an understatement.

I'll be in a mental facility for the rest of my life, I think.

I'm not sure what's worse, this or prison.

I was told my 'condition' is no excuse for criminal activity.

Shocker.

Either way, I'll be flip-flopping like a fish between the criminal justice system and the mental health system for the rest of my pathetic life.

Of course I plead not guilty by reason of insanity. I had to.

How could I possibly be culpable when I didn't know I was doing it, right?!

The public was outraged.

River is with Cody now.

He wants to visit me with her but at this stage, it's not allowed. On the other hand, unsurprisingly, Robyn does not want to visit me. Who can blame her, after what I did to her.

I miss her, when I'm Piper. She doesn't understand that I think; doesn't understand that sometimes I still want to destroy her.

That's the thing about Dissociative Identity Disorder, there's no magic pill to take it away.

Nothing can get rid of who I can become.

I can talk to the doctors as much as I want and do their stupid exercises, but I'll never escape the people living inside of me. When they take over, I cannot help.

I am a prisoner in my own body.

So perhaps it's a good thing that I'm paralysed now.

It certainly makes everyone around me feel safer.

The 'Robyn's' inside of me didn't plan for things to go this way. Everything just spiralled out of control.

I guess it's like that with everything in life though.

No matter how hard you try to control a situation, life has other plans and nothing you do can stop them.

I hear Cody tried to start a petition for me. Free Piper! So sweet. Forever loyal, that one.

Why do I always go for the bad boys?

Cody would have been so much better for me, upon reflection.

Anyway, I don't think he got many signatures on his petition, if any.

Not many people think my current situation is quite as

controversial as Cody does.
The world hates me and now I guess that is my cross to bear.
I touch the scar on my neck. It's thick and lumpy.
A constant reminder.
For the rest of time, I will be remembered as The Piroutte
Predator.

They're saying I must have definitely had an accomplice, that I
couldn't possibly have done it all on my own.
Perhaps that is true.
Perhaps it is not.
Try as they might, the cops will never get the truth out of me.

Epilogue

Robyn

It's been seven months since Piper was caught.
It has been the most bizarre seven months of my life that, before this, was really quite dull.

It took me a while, but I'm back at the school teaching again.
I have a gift, you see.
Retelling stories through song and dance is my passion.
I couldn't ignore it for too long.
It did break my heart when I realised I'd never be able to dance again. Not after losing my toes. I had no chance.
I still keep my beaten up pointe shoes strung up in the cottage.
Sometimes I sit and stare at them for hours, reminiscing on a different life.
I run my hand across my old ballet bar, remembering the feeling of dancing. The feeling of waiting in the wings of the stage, watching the curtain slowly lift to reveal my audience.
All eyes on me as I glide to centre-stage.
It was like a drug to me.
My balance has gone now.

I have hardly any strength left.
You'd hardly notice though, not when I put on my custom shoes.
Not quite as alluring as ballet slippers, are they?
I have 'toe fillers' now. I swear if you told me a year ago that this is where my life would be today, I'd have laughed at you.

The shoes are a help, but it will never be the same.
My relationship with Piper will never be the same again either.
The way she looked at me while she was slicing off my toes down in that basement will haunt me for the rest of my life.
It was like she didn't even know who I was.
To her, I was just like all the other girls in the room.
I wasn't her twin sister.
I was nobody.
Maybe to her, I always was.
I've come to accept my fate, I suppose.
Those that can't do, teach, as they say.

I'm working on a new ballet production at the moment.
Giselle never went ahead. No one felt quite right picking that show back up.
The ghostly maiden costumes I'd worked tirelessly on for months have been stored away, collecting dust in the dressing room.
I have a new class of fresh dancers now. New talent.
We're creating our own version of Coppélia.
We decided to go for a comic ballet production this time.
No one really wanted to do something too serious after everything that transpired over the last few months.
It's a story about a man who notices this incredibly beautiful woman sitting by her window reading a book.
Try as he might, he can't seem to get her attention. He falls hopelessly in love with her even though he's engaged to be married to another woman.
Little does he know that she is actually a life-sized doll, created by a mad scientist who had put her out to dry. The scientist is trying to find a way to bring the doll to life and make her his life

companion.

Regardless, the man is besotted with this woman with her face buried in a book.

His fiancée notices how infatuated he is with her, learns that she's actually a doll and starts to impersonate her to win over her true love.

As silly as the story sounds, the choreography is still incredible.

I'm having fun with it. Getting to know my new students... every one of them has their own story and I'm loving learning the new dynamics of this group.

Everyone has a secret; and I am slowly figuring them all out.

Day by day, I'm slowly starting to feel a little bit like me again.

I've started a support group with all of the girls who I was kept down in the basement with.

We're all dealing with major post traumatic stress as I'm sure you can imagine.

It's good that we have each other.

We're all cut from the same cloth now. Dancers who can't dance. Mutilated. Broken.

Having them to fall back on is like a safety net for me, and they all trust me. Despite my appearance, looking just like Piper, they think I'm different because I went through exactly what they went to.

It's a wonderfully unique situation.

I have night terrors sometimes, you know. I wake up seeing Piper's face, *my* face, staring at me.

I'm on so much medication now, but still sleep eludes me.

I've taken up smoking now, too. Since I can't dance anymore, I thought, fuck it. Why not?

I'd found Piper's cigarettes in her handbag and it felt so natural putting one of them between my lips for the first time.

I put one between my lips now and light it up, thinking about the day ahead.

I'm supposed to be meeting up with the girls later but I'm just not sure I'm up to it.

Some days are better than others.

The baby gurgles sleepily as she wakes up.
I look down at this little bundle in my arms. Her baby.
I hear that some days Piper doesn't even remember having her.
How do you just forget nine months of pregnancy?
How do you forget the birth?
How do you forget holding your child in your arms for the very first time?
It's not like she has dementia or something.
Is it possible that throughout her whole pregnancy and birth that Piper was someone else?
I don't know how Dissociative Identity Disorder works. I'm too scared to find out.
Being pregnant while paralysed caused so many problems for her. I didn't want to hear about all of the issues at first. The urinary tract infections and pressure sores. The confusion. Some days she'd wake up and have no idea why her stomach was so huge.
I wasn't even sure why I was secretly checking in with the nurses to see how she was.
I guess that even after everything she did to me, she'll always be my twin sister.
Our bond, at the end of the day, is unbreakable.
No one will ever understand that.
Our DNA is identical. We are the result of one fertilized egg. One. We are one.
She is special to me – I can't deny that.
I stroke my finger down the baby's nose. It's covered in tiny milk spots.
She gives me a gummy smile, her cleft chin covered in drool.
I smile back down at her, brushing her golden curls to one side.
Love swells from deep inside of me.
Tests still need to be done to find out if she's Cody's or Luke's.
My guess is Luke's.
She has his long lashes and azure eyes. As blue as the sky.
I guess that's why Piper chose that name for her.

Sky.

She's too beautiful for words.

Piper's pregnancy was a shock to everyone.

She'd been on birth control, but who knows if she was taking it consistently or not. She certainly wasn't consistent with her other medication – but a baby was the last thing any of us expected.

She's a little miracle, really.

She's the softest, purest thing I have ever come across.

I don't think anyone knows what innocence is until they hold a newborn baby for the first time.

I don't really know what drove Piper into wanting to keep the baby, if I'm honest. She knew it would be taken from her almost immediately.

All it took was one look at it and I was in love.

It must have been Luke's eyes that did it. I still love him so much. I told them I'd look after her.

She reminds me of him.

She's my little piece of him to hold on to now that he's gone.

Sometimes I imagine that she's my baby with Luke. Not my sisters baby. That's how it was supposed to be.

I know it's selfish of me to think that way.

There are other reasons I decided to keep Sky too, I swear.

I mean, how could I subject this tiny, defenceless little human to a childhood in foster homes when I know just how bad they can be?

When I looked down at her and saw Luke's eyes staring right back at me full of dependence, I knew I would give her absolutely everything that I'd never had as a child.

Piper told me not to visit her.

She told me to stay away, pretend to hate her.

It was the only way.

People need to trust me, she said.

Now I don't know if it was *her* talking at all.

I don't even know if she *remembers* the plan.

Down in that basement I honestly thought she was going to kill me.

With everything she said and told me to do, I just decided to nod my head and agree with everything.

I know it was crazy but I was just trying to stay alive.

But then, through time, being down in that basement and seeing her every day... I just saw my sister again. Tortured and lost, yes. But still my sister.

Perhaps you can call it Stockholm Syndrome.

I don't really know what it is that I have.

All I know is that, just like her, I have blackouts too.

We are twins, after all.

We're more alike than anyone knows.

Obviously I won't tell anybody that. It would ruin everything.

I can't afford to arouse any suspicion.

Even if Piper doesn't remember our plan, I need to see it through.

No one can stop me now.

Jade Lee Wright is a former everything-ist. A jack of all trades. A globe trotter. A hopeless romantic. A true crime addict. Podcaster. Ukelele strummer. Bookworm. Beach bum. Surfer. Terrible artist. An even worse crocheter. A pretty good cook. Massive foodie. Lover of wine. Would rather be camping than in a luxury hotel.

God knows where she is in the world right now. It's constantly changing.

If you ever meet her, tell her to write a better About The Author page.

Printed in Great Britain
by Amazon

46517994R00113